The
Odyssey of
Ben O'Neal

The Odyssey of Ben O'Neal

Theodore Taylor

An Odyssey/Harcourt Young Classic

Harcourt, Inc.

Orlando   Austin   New York   San Diego   Toronto   London

www.HarcourtBooks.com

First Harcourt Young Classics edition 2004
First Odyssey Classics edition 2004
First published by Doubleday and Company, Inc. 1977
First paperback edition published by Avon Books 1979

Library of Congress Cataloging-in-Publication Data
Taylor, Theodore, 1921–
The odyssey of Ben O'Neal/by Theodore Taylor.
p. cm.
"The Cape Hatteras Trilogy."
Sequel to: Teetoncey and Ben O'Neal.
Summary: The further adventures of Ben and Teetoncey as they take to the
sea—he, to find his brother, and she, to escape a forced return to England.
[1. Sea stories.] I. Title.
PZ7.T2186Od 2004
[Fic]—dc22   2003067705
ISBN 0-15-205299-2
ISBN 0-15-205295-X pb

Text set in Dante
Designed by Lydia D'moch

Printed in the United States of America

A C E G H F D B
A C E G H F D B (pb)

For Brandy Golden Boy,
dog of Wendy Lynn and hound about the house,
model for the mule-headed character of "Boo"

Laguna Beach, California
September 1975

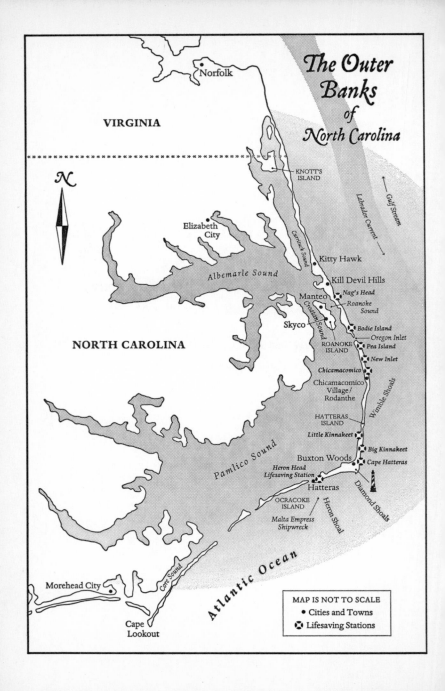

The Outer Banks of North Carolina

VIRGINIA

Norfolk

KNOTT'S ISLAND

Elizabeth City

Albemarle Sound

Curtuck Sound

Kitty Hawk

Kill Devil Hills

Nag's Head

Manteo

Roanoke Sound

Skyco

Croatan Sound

NORTH CAROLINA

Bodie Island

Oregon Inlet

ROANOKE ISLAND

Pea Island

New Inlet

Chicamacomico

Chicamacomico Village / Rodanthe

Wimble Shoals

HATTERAS ISLAND

Little Kinnakeet

Big Kinnakeet

Buxton Woods

Cape Hatteras

Heron Head Lifesaving Station

Hatteras

Diamond Shoals

Pamlico Sound

OCRACOKE ISLAND

Malta Empress Shipwreck

Heron Shoal

Labrador Current

Gulf Stream

Morehead City

Core Sound

Atlantic Ocean

Cape Lookout

MAP IS NOT TO SCALE
● Cities and Towns
✪ Lifesaving Stations

The
Odyssey of
Ben O'Neal

I

THERE IS A trusted saying on our remote Outer
Banks of North Carolina that we who live there
are all frail children of the moody Mother Sea,
that she watches over and controls our every des-
tiny. Shapes us as she carves out sandbars. Puts
us in raging waves or calm, sunny waters. Makes
fools out of us now and then, and isn't beyond
having a good laugh herself. However, in her behalf, the old people claim she takes a long and
careful time before making up her mind on how
to dispose of us. She'll beckon us mysteriously

when she's ready and not a tide before. There is also steadfast belief from Kill Devil Hills clear to Hatteras village and Ocracoke Island that she talks to us constantly and often we don't listen.

I do believe that now, although I didn't pay it much attention in March 1899, when my various voyages began. The Mother Sea was having a good laugh for herself during that trying period.

In the chill, gray dawn of a Tuesday, in the midmonth, sun reddening but not yet mounting the horizon, I stood at the dew-coated rail on the quivering stern of the steamer *Neuse*, looking south down Croatan Sound, which lies between Roanoke Island, of Lost Colony fame, and the flat, marshy Carolina mainland. Below my feet, glassy bubbles and white froth boiled out from the railway ferry as she throbbed steadily toward the Pasquotank River and Elizabeth City, North Carolina, where a train would be waiting to carry me on to Norfolk, across the Virginia border.

A knowledgeable but plotting girl once told me my face smacked poetically of sun on Irish bogs and Land's End winters. I can't at all vouch for that, but I can tell you how I looked that Tuesday otherwise. I was clad in a sturdy brown wool jacket, good knickers, black stockings without holes in them, and a seaman's blue wool cap (courtesy of surfman Mark Jennette), and by my legs rested a tubby canvas bag containing clothes, a pair of rubber boots, writing paper, a towel, and a bar of soap. So far as I knew, I was well equipped for what lay ahead but not so well off for what lay behind.

Way down the sound I could still make out the little boat's sails but could no longer see the comforting, hunched forms of Keeper Filene Midgett and surfman Jabez Tillett. Already they were beating away in the sharpie, and in late afternoon would arrive at Chicky Dock, on the Pamlico Sound. The Outer Banks, a string of small islands with low dunes and hammocks, bent oaks and scrub holly, flank the sounds, with a watching and listening and talking Atlantic Ocean on the other side, to east. Without doubt, Filene and Jabez would be safely to home at Heron Head Lifesaving Station, which Keeper

Midgett commanded, well before supper of wild pig or Mattamuskeet deer or roast ruddy duck, over which to talk about the event of the morning: my great departure.

Home, I couldn't help but think. With people they knew. Places they knew. Standing there, I shivered, I remember, and it wasn't from any icy wind. Disgraceful tears, once more (and I was certainly glad that the men in the sharpie hadn't seen them), had stopped. I'd resolutely fought them back, but somehow my throat kept on crowding. Only ten minutes before, when the *Neuse* pulled away from the dock at Skyco, Filene and Jabez had let the sharpie drift on out into the channel, then waved a last farewell before hauling sail up.

Never would they know just how close I'd come to yelling, "Take me with you."

A few minutes later, with three miles of brown water already separating the sailboat from the high-stacked white steamer, I thought very hard about turning myself around in Elizabeth City, swallowing my pride as I was gulping the gummy throat lumps, admit I was scared right down to my high-top shoes. Go home and unpack my seabag and wait in the small shingle house near Heron Head for brother Reuben to return from his voyages in the Caribbean.

I also distinctly recall hoping I'd see that sharpie come smartly about and race after the *Neuse,* finally catching it in Lizzie City, big Cousin Filene shouting up, "I been thinkin', Ben. You ought to wait to next year, when you're fourteen. Come on down an' git in this boat with us . . ."

It didn't happen, of course.

Then I tried to imagine what they were saying to each other and later found out I wasn't the width of six hairs off.

FILENE: "I do deceive that boy may be tougher'n John O'Neal. Didn't leak nary a tear. Jus' stood there manly an' said good-bye. For sure, he is tougher'n Reuben. Why, the night his mama died, if he cried I didn't see it. He jus' took off south on that pony o' his."

Well, I cried plentysome.

FILENE: "But a dozen times this week I felt like tellin' Ben he shouldn't go. Too quick after his mama died. Too soon to git his feet wet. He should stay with us up to the station, or up to the Odens or Farrows or Gillikins, an' they all thought about offerin'. . . ."

I would have refused and they all knew it. I'd talked too bragging much about going out to sea; dug my own foolish pit, so to speak.

FILENE: "Thirteen's a mite young to go to open sea, but Ben could always rightfully tell us that his brother had done it no older'n that. Others on the Banks afore him."

JABEZ: "That is true, Cap'n. I did myself." Jabez often took a big spit of Ashe's best plug after he said something profound and undoubtedly did this time.

FILENE: "As I do recall, Reuben was not a month over thirteen when he went off to Norfolk. I remember that Rachel, God rest her soul, was beside herself."

JABEZ: "That she was. I don't think it happened more'n a year after John O'Neal capsized."

FILENE: "About then. But I think John O'Neal, God rest his heroic soul, too, would have been right proud today that he had a boy who'd buried his dead an' faced the wind."

JABEZ: "Right proud." And then a six-to-eight-foot spit.

In truth, I wasn't facing the wind, and the region between my chin and forehead must have looked like a wrung-out mop.

I stayed by the rail until the peak of canvas vanished behind the first sun rays and then made my way toward the bow, pausing outside the lounging and dining saloon. It was richly carpeted in red, everything clean and shining. Forward were two long tables with snowy cloths, silver-colored cream pitchers, and thin little rose vases, minus roses because it wasn't summer as yet.

Other passengers were already eating breakfast. The coffee smelled good, as did the frying pork belly. So, carrying my seabag inside, placing it down where I could watch it—Filene had warned of thieves north of Kitty Hawk—I advanced on one table and sat down at the far end, away from other diners. Looking around that saloon, I'd never seen such splendor.

In a moment, a tall, elderly waiter in a starched white SS *Neuse* jacket with brass buttons on it placed a glass of water in front of me and said pleasantly, "Mornin'. We got some nice Smithfield ham today. Or some Philadelphy scrapple. Virginia trout. Grits 'n' gravy."

From strain, my voice cracked when I answered. "Reckon I'll have some oatmeal, please." More and more, my vocal cords were doing that of late, the usual plague of change of life.

Almost without thinking of it, I touched my pants pocket to see if the odd change was still there; let my hand slip stealthily to my breastbone to feel the fourteen dollars, my entire fund, bound tightly and hanging on a whistle lanyard, an idea of Filene's. It was safely there.

I'd seen these steam railway ferries many times as they plied the sounds and had boarded this same vessel once, just recently, when delivering Teetoncey, the British shipwreck survivor who'd lost her parents and was headed back for

London, England. But I'd never been a passenger myself and had no idea what they charged for breakfast. Oatmeal shouldn't be more than a few pennies, anywhere.

"No ham 'n' eggs?" asked the waiter, tempting me.

"Just some oatmeal, please," I replied, feeling hot and stuffy.

"Shame we got no berries today," said the waiter, moving off toward the galley.

Thirty minutes later, I was down on the second deck of the *Neuse*, leaning out of an open cargo port near the stern, throwing up. There was hardly a ripple on the Albemarle Sound and I could only guess that the sour gush of porridge wasn't exactly from seasickness.

2

THE FOLLOWING will not be of much interest to lucky people who travel trains often, but I must tell it all exactly as it happened.

Lizzie City, North Carolina, with streetlights and brick buildings and more stores and people than I ever knew existed, was most impressive but did not compare to the mud-colored four coaches and baggage car of the Elizabeth City & Norfolk Railroad, Currituck line, as they sat behind an engine that made a heavy, metallic breathing sound. Though I wouldn't have cared to admit it to any living soul, never before had my eyes chanced upon a real train. I let them slowly travel the length of the busy platform, staying a long time on the engine. Just like the pictures in *McClure's Monthly*, all right.

I had my confidence back. The fear and loneliness of an hour before had pretty much given way to pure excitement. Except for hollowness, my heaving stomach had settled down and I was beginning to believe I'd make it. Finally, I climbed the EC&N steps into the first coach, having a little trouble with my seabag. It almost knocked the hat off a fat lady following behind. But it was a very large hat. "Watch it, boy," she snapped, and I duly apologized, only to graze her again a few feet down the aisle.

"Will you settle somewhere," she said, with unbridled annoyance. City people are short on both manners and forgiveness, I soon learned.

"Yes, ma'am," I replied, feeling very awkward, all fumbling hands and feet, but also thinking that women on the Banks were never this jumpy, not even Mavis Gillikin, who often had spells of twitching nerves.

Shoving the seabag onto a seat, I quickly

pushed in behind it as the fat lady passed along with a snort and a searing look. No sooner had that happened when the man across the way leaned over. "Son, your bag is supposed to go back with the luggage or else put it under your seat." I felt foolish twice again but stowed it promptly.

Just getting on the train is a considerably vexing chore, I discovered. But looking around, I'd never viewed such a fancy thing on wheels; far nicer than Reuben had described. The seats were padded and upholstered in nubby green. There were overhead electric lights; heating pipes ran down near the floor.

Then everything happened at once. The conductor yelled, "All aboard." There was a slight jerk; then another, and I found myself holding my breath as the cars moved, a deep chomping sound coming from up ahead, creaking sounds from beneath. So this was how Reuben did it so long ago. For years, walking over the sand trails on the Banks, or in bed at night, I'd thought about this very day, and now it was here, suddenly spinning along. The station and the platform disappeared and the land began to rush by.

A few minutes later, nose pressed against the window so as not to miss anything, I barely heard the conductor calling for tickets, and frantically searched around the seat. He stood over me and laughed. "It's in your hand."

Clearly, I made a terrible mess of things that first twenty minutes, and it took another twenty to work up courage for something else I'd planned for a long time. I rose up, keeping my eyes strictly ahead, and went to the narrow mahogany door at the rear of the car, opened it, and stepped into the cubicle, locking the door securely behind me. For a moment, I just stood there in awe, looking down at the flush toilet, then up to the water chamber with the brass pull chain. An outhouse on wheels! And I promptly unbuttoned my pants to partake of the luxury.

A moment later, I could hardly contain a shout of triumph as I reached for the iron knob on the chain. Holding the lid up, I watched joyfully as the water spewed down to the crossties of the roadbed. What an event!

It was the first of my many experiences with modern conveniences, and I went back down the aisle as if I'd ridden a train a thousand times. Unfortunately, I did not fool one unkind railway employee.

Just after we crossed the Virginia border, other side of Moyock, a harsh voice came thrusting up behind me. "Candy bars! Cookies! Apples! Pears!"

Hovering near was a skinny, oval-faced, green-eyed boy in a baggy brown uniform, hat with a shiny plate saying ATLANTIC NEWS COMPANY on his head, blond hair spiking out from under it. In the crook of his long arm was a laden wicker basket ringed with chocolate bars.

Suddenly realizing I was now hungry, I said, "I'll take an apple."

The boy rested the basket on the seat arm. "You pick it. That'll be five cents."

"Five cents?" I was stunned, though the apples were certainly larger and shinier than any I'd ever seen. But fine winesaps sold for a penny each at the Burrus store, in Chicky village, where I'd previously worked; plucking chickens, packing ducks in ice, head down; errands and such.

"That's robbery," I said, withdrawing my hand.

He eyed me coldly. "You wanted to buy it."

"I don't now."

The boy looked me over as if examining a possum held by the tail. "Where you goin'?"

"Bound out to sea."

He hooted. "To sea? You ain't old enough to sail bathtub boats."

Well, despite the fact that he was trying to grow a mustache and doing a scraggly poor job of it, he didn't look a day over fifteen himself. Worse, he talked with a Yankee twang. Yet I couldn't help but be impressed with him. Here he was on these trains day after day. A merchant, no less. So, deepening my tone as much as I could, I looked the skinny peddler straight in the eye. "I'm old enough, all right. Seventeen."

The boy grinned, balancing with the sway of the coach. "You a captain?"

"No," I replied. "Just a sailor," I added, holding my temper.

"You been to sea before?"

"Many times." The Pamlico, on to which our rickety dock extended, was a sea of sorts.

The insolent grin vanished. "Tar Heel, I don't even think you been on a train till today."

Embarrassed, I looked around. Some of the other passengers were listening. The man across the way was laughing.

"I watched you," the vicious seller went on. "Your mouth was wide open when you boarded in Lizzie City. I've seen hundreds like you. Real hayseeds."

I felt fire spreading over my cheeks as he tipped his hat and went on down the aisle yelling about his apples and pears.

3

THE TRAIN RUMBLED along over the marshy land, whistling at last at Brand Creek Turnpike, slowing to curve around at Chatham Junction and begin the run directly east to Union Station. A few minutes later, I saw the outskirts of the city, marred with smoke, and a dryness came into my throat. Scared again. Houses, no more than twenty or thirty feet apart, and streets, some paved, stretched in every direction. A trolley car—and I'd heard of them—went by an intersection and the train curved widely, slowing and whistling, as other tracks suddenly sprouted alongside.

I wiped at drops of sweat as the conductor came down the aisle yelling, "Nor-fawk, Nor-fawk . . ." The moment of trial was near on that fourteenth day of March.

Finally, the train jerked to a stop by a long shed and I did what everyone else was doing: got off. Passengers threaded by me, baggage carts were rolling, and I finally moved with the throng, bewildered and bumping about.

Inside the depot, I looked around, peered up at the high ceiling, gandered all the people going in different directions, not quite certain what to do next. Then, remembering that Reuben had said there was a place called Sailor's Bethany in Norfolk where you could get sleep for thirty cents a night, I prepared to make inquiry on how to get there, when up walked that insolent apple seller from the train.

"You lost?" he asked.

I came very near saying toughly, "Mind your

own Yankee business," but my knees were on the verge of knocking. So I replied, "I'd like to get to Sailor's Bethany. It's somewhere here. Maybe down on the waterfro-*ont*." Of all miserable luck, my voice squeaked again.

The boy stood there lordly and cocked his head over. "Tar Heel, you been to sea so many times you ought to find it easy." The green eyes prodded.

Plainly, I had two choices. Tell him the gospel truth or wander around stupidly asking other people. Again looking at him straight, I admitted, "First time on a train; first time to sea, if I can get there." I felt vast relief.

The boy grinned and pushed back his Atlantic News Company hat. "First time away from home, too, I figure. Name's Michael Grant." He shoved his hand out.

He was friendly, after all, I thought, quite surprised. "Mine's Ben O'Neal. I'm from down Hatteras way." His thin hand was firm and just as friendly. I had misjudged the Yankee boy.

"Wherever you're from, you don't want to

stay at Sailor's Bethany. Despite all the soul-savin', too many drunks there every night. To-morrow morning you won't have that seabag, either. Maybe not your shoes."

"My older brother stayed there."

"How old's he?"

"Twenty-four."

"How old are you?"

There was no sense in carrying on the lie at this point. "Thirteen."

"Ben, you got a lot to learn about cities. Those men might not tamper with your big brother, but they'll backhand you quicker'n look at you. I should know. I've rescued a dozen like you. I been drummin' two years."

"Drummin'?"

"Sellin' on these trains. I been to Norfolk a hundred times."

I could not hide my curiosity. "How old are you, Mike?"

"Sixteen come May."

Yet he seemed much older, now that we were talking about something other than overpriced apples. "All right, where should I go?"

"Come to a safe place. My boardinghouse. Mrs. Crowe's. I sleep there overnight, and keep my street clothes in a closet when I don't."

"How much does she charge?"

"Sixty-five cents a night, including breakfast and supper."

"I can't afford that," I protested. Me and Mama had lived on five dollars a month in the house near Heron Head. My fund, which was already damaged by the railway fare, would be gone in three weeks at those outrageous prices.

"There're lice-ridden places here you can get a bed for fifteen cents, but watch they don't slit your throat during the night. Besides, you got to buy all your meals extra."

All this talk about getting backhanded and slit-throated was unnerving. "I guess I better go with you."

We walked out to East Main Street and headed for midtown. Buildings were jawbone to jawbone, some five stories high. Trolley tracks were in the middle of the street. Horse wagons jangled by. People moved along the sidewalk like schooled fish.

Mike wagged his head to one side. "Chinese places."

HOP SING & COMPANY SHING HONG YICK SAM I had never seen a Chinese, dead or alive, and looked into the window of Hop Sing, smelling herbs, making up my mind to come back and walk this street slowly.

"This is purely the biggest street I ever saw," I confessed, craning my head, almost stumbling several times. The signs alone were enough to stop a person: MUTUAL LIFE INSURANCE OF NEW YORK WESTERN UNION TELEGRAPH COMPANY POCOMOKE GUANO COMPANY COLUMBIA TYPEWRITER COMPANY FEREBEE, JONES & COMPANY, AGENTS FOR KNOX HATS.

To think all these things were going on less than two hundred miles from Chicky Dock.

NORFOLK CONSERVATORY OF MUSIC NORFOLK SHAVING PARLOR HEPTASOPHIAN HALL, whatever that was.

"Has to be the biggest street in the world," I said.

Mike shook his head. "Only seventy-one miles

22

of streets in this town. Some made of Belgian blocks, some cobblestone, some brick. Some just ground oyster shells. Wait'll you see Philadelphia and New York. This is a hick town."

Hick town? He should visit Whalebone, North Carolina.

A trolley came ringing by, spraying sparks, and I almost fell into the gutter, trying to walk backward and watch it.

Mike smiled. "Stay around here long enough and you'll see some steam automobiles."

"Automobiles?" Impossible.

"Run on banana oil. Electric trucks, too."

I couldn't wait to see them. "You from New York, Mike?"

"No, Scranton. That's in Pennsylvania."

Thankfully, he wasn't from Baltimore, which Filene had said was full of criminals. But he was solid Yankee, all right, though he seemed to be a nice enough one. They had played hod down toward Hatteras during the war, cutting timber as if they owned it, and were still unwelcome south of Moyock. If anything, I was solid Confederate, and Robert E. Lee, not General Grant, was my idea of a hero. But bygones had to be bygones.

As we walked on, I listened to the city. There seemed to be constant harsh noise in the streets, so different from the Banks. Far off, I could hear the yallowing of steamships and tug whistles in the river reaches, and I noticed the smells. Food and coal smoke and fertilizer and tar and creosote and roasting coffee beans. Pleasing anti-septic smells that pushed out of open doors along-side windows edged in brass. Robert Holmes, Druggist, was at No. 196, with a white tile floor; selling medicines, toilet articles, and Whitman's Fine Candies; advertising a new Tuff Revier double-stand soda-water fountain of solid onyx and overhead wooden-paddle electric fans.

All of it was overwhelming.

We made headway up on Main, then twisted and turned and soon arrived at a tall white house that was on a lane off a street called Granby.

4

Surrounded by strangers, I felt somewhat ill at ease at supper and ate mostly in silence, sitting by Mike Grant, listening and looking nonetheless. Red-haired Mrs. Crowe, who said she usually had no truck with riffraff from the sea, though she made an exception in my case, was rather small and quick; peppery of speech and sharp of light blue eye, independent enough for a widow of forty-five left with a fourteen-room house and not much else. Most of her middle-aged boarders were talkative railroad men, as had been her late husband, I soon learned.

I also quickly discovered that Mrs. Crowe, a dedicated Baptist, had a certain reputation in downtown Norfolk. Prominent member of the local Woman's Christian Temperance Union, she often burst into East Main Street saloons to kneel by the bar and shout, "Deliver them from Satan." When she was really stirred up, she broke bottles and poured the poison into spittoons.

She also had her rigid rules in the narrow four-story house fronted by a nice porch with scrollwork and round supporting posties, lined with six green rocking chairs. The rules were posted in every room and I read them, but none applied to me, of course.

- WHISKEY BREATH IS STRICTLY PROHIBITED.
- NO BEDROOM SLIPPERS ALLOWED IN THE DINING ROOM.
- NO FEMALE BOARDERS (BECAUSE THEY WASH THEIR BLOOMERS AND HANG THEM OUT THE WINDOW).
- NO PETS.

- CIGARS AND PIPES PERMITTED AFTER DESSERT. NO ASHES IN THE FERNERY.
- NO SMOKING IN BED.

So far as housekeeping goes, in a way she reminded me of fussbudgety Filene Midgett. She presided like a banty peacock at the table of nine that cool, clear evening over platters of ham hocks and new potatoes, fried lightly; bowls of black-eyed peas, and a warmer of buttermilk biscuits.

The talk was railroad talk, and I had never heard it before. High-wheeled Atlantic locomotives and air brakes and automatic couplers. No. 999 had pulled the Empire State Express at more than a hundred miles an hour in '93, and there was no reason not to get that kind of engine on the Norfolk & Western tracks and pull hotshot freights, said Mr. Stone, brakeman on a coal train.

"Shush, Mr. Stone," ordered Mrs. Crowe to the bald, big-jowled man who wore lavender galluses. "I want to talk to this innocent boy."

My mind was already weary from the wear and tear of the day, but Mrs. Crowe was never to be denied.

"Now, I say you'd be much better off going to work in the N&W machine shop out at Lambert's Point. They hire apprentices and treat them well. In five years you can be running a lathe or making molds. Earn a decent living without the temptations of the sea."

They were all waiting for my answer, looking at me. Finally, I explained, "I have to go to sea, ma'am."

"And who is forcing you to do that?"

"I expect I am," I replied, as earnestly as I could. "It's in my family blood."

"You should drain it out."

The railroad men laughed.

"I can't, ma'am."

In fact, it was Reuben who had talked about that glorious moment when the last line separates from the dock and the ship becomes a world of its own; that moment when it lifts on the first ocean swell, outbound. "I just can't do it," I repeated.

Mrs. Crowe let out an exasperated sigh and tapped a fork by her plate in annoyance. She did not like to be overruled. "Well, if you must go on and expose yourself to the most wicked people on earth, you go to J. M. Jordan's in the morning and tell him Ethel Crowe sent you. He's a fine Christian man, honest as a creek pebble, and won't steer you to a hellship."

J. M. Jordan's. I nodded gratefully. I'd heard of Jordan's, the foremost ship chandlers. They provisioned vessels, supplying food and all manner of things.

"Moreover, I suppose you'll enjoy listening to sea stories around his Heatrola, hot or cold, though I wouldn't give a whit for a sea story. Sailors are all terrible liars as well as drunks. But all the best captains come to Jordan's, over Oscar Smith or D. S. Baum."

Reuben had mentioned Jordan's, and that Heatrola, a big, barrel-like stove, come to think of it. I thanked her kindly.

Mrs. Crowe then nodded permission to Mr. Stone, who resumed his discussion of fast locomotives to pull hotshot freights on the N&W line.

After dessert, of hot peach dumplings doused with thick cream, Mrs. Crowe cleared the table, served coffee, opened the windows to let smoke out, and retired to the kitchen with a curt warning to drop no ashes on the parlor rug and a reminder to me to "think about it."

"I will, ma'am," I promised.

Twilight had spread over the port.

Red and green running lights, white mast lights, were moving around the branches of the Elizabeth River, hulls almost hidden in the gloom, though the ship whistles and tugboat toots from the harbor were not as frequent now.

Six bells, seven o'clock, was rung down on the ships as Mike and I paused briefly on the fourth-floor landing, which had a wide window affording a good view.

"That's Portsmouth over there, and the ferries dock here at the foot of Commercial. Those are the Merchant & Miner docks down there. Old Bay Line. Over there is the naval hospital."

Paddle-wheel ferries, their walking beams rocking like steel seesaws, churned the water between

Portsmouth and Commercial Street. Small boats crisscrossed the wakes, bucking and plunging. Almost dead ahead of us, a white vessel, aglow in every window and port, moved slowly upriver.

"She's from the nation's capital. Norfolk & Washington Steamboat Company. They dock at the foot of Water."

She blew hoarsely as a small oyster dredger crossed her bow.

Ah, the life in a bustling port city, I thought, my feet almost floating up with contentment. On the morrow there go I, were my thoughts.

In the room, Mike settled down and lit up a white clay pipe, giving me the notion that I might possibly want to spend some money on a pipe and sack of tobacco. It would make me seem older, I concluded. With my lifelong companions on the Banks, Kilbie Oden and Frank Scarborough, I had tried tobacco, both the shredded kind and chewing plug, with not much instant pleasure and some later illness. Yet sitting there and puffing, Mike looked very mature.

"Sure you don't want to think about that N&W machine shop? Mrs. Crowe knows the foreman."

I shook my head. "Made up my mind this morning on the *Neuse* to try and find Reuben down in the Caribbean. He's my big brother, mate on a brig running between Trinidad, the Barbadoes, and Port Fernandino. That's in Florida. He doesn't even know Mama's dead."

"No one else left in your family except him?"

"Not a soul. Papa died a long time ago. Then brother Guthrie. Mama died last month."

Smoke rose and eddied into Mike's blond hair as he turned solemn and thoughtful. "My old man just as well be dead. He gets paid noontime Saturday an' drinks till sundown Sunday. He used to beat up on all of us. That's mainly why I left home. Worked as kitchen boy at the Vanderbilt in New York City first."

I shook my head sympathetically and sat down on the edge of the bed, hoping I could stay a while. "I never knew my papa."

Mike laughed hollowly. "I wish I'd never known mine."

That wasn't a nice thing to say and I wanted to change the subject but didn't do a very good job of it. "You ever get homesick?"

There was thick silence a moment. "Sometimes. I spent Christmas Day between New Bern and Lizzie City. Five passengers on that whole train. We slowed down for little towns and I could see people that morning in their front rooms opening their presents ... trees with candles on them ..."

I suddenly felt sorry for this boy.

"You'll get that way, too, believe me," Mike said, green eyes warning. "It'll hit you when you least expect it. One thing, you can always go back home and no one will slap you or cuss you."

No one ever did that, I recalled. Never.

Mike went on with the distressing subject. "I can't remember when there wasn't meanness in my house. Even my brother and sister turned mean."

I could not remember a single time when Rachel O'Neal was really mean. Oh, she was cantankerous now and then; nagged now and then. Always jumpy about me going near the water. But never mean. "I guess I had a good house after all," I said, wishing we hadn't gotten onto this subject this particular evening.

"Lucky you didn't get born in mine," Mike said.

I told him about our house and a sand pony and dog I'd had, but he wouldn't talk about his house. He did mention his dog, Burnie, rescued from a stable fire. Not much else.

For a painful moment, a clear picture of our house, tucked at the end of a pathway in red myrtle, scrub holly, and live oak, popped into my mind. Then the faces of Mama, Filene, Jabez, Mark Jennette; Kilbie, Frank, and Mr. Burrus, even surly Hardie Miller, passed before me. I found myself getting clog-throated and said, "We knew everybody, just like family."

"Maybe you should have stayed on and waited for your brother."

What an untimely thing for him to say: I looked at him and struggled with that idea again, not that I hadn't been struggling with it since early morning. I pushed it back and tried to clear my mind. "But, stuck out on those Banks, sometimes I went crazy, Mike. You ever seen them?"

"Closest I ever got was Lizzie City."

"Sand and shipwrecks. Lifesaving stations. Not much else. No roads, no electricity, no chamber toilets. You could put Chicky village, Clarks, Buxton, and Hatteras in four square blocks of what I saw today."

Mike nodded. "I still might trade you for Scranton."

I blew a breath. "I don't know what got into me yesterday. I took a look around just before I left and it didn't look so bad . . ."

"Hmh," said Mike.

I hit the bedspread with the palm of my hand. "Tell me about trains, Mike . . ."

He did, but somehow we got back to Heron Head and, nearing ten o'clock, Mike said to me, "Well, Heron Head sounds a lot better'n Scranton."

That was hard to believe. "Yeah, but you're out of Scranton now, riding these trains every day. You been everywhere, New York and Philadelphia . . ."

He nodded but got up and went over to the window. When he turned back, I could not understand the look on his face. It seemed dark and empty. "I guess . . ." Then he walked back over and grasped the counterpane up by the pillow. "I'm tired of talking."

Just like an adult, I thought. Exactly like one.

"I'm sleepy, that's all, Ben," he said, an edge still in his voice.

"See you in the morning," I said, mystified by his change of mood, all clouded over in seconds.

"If you're up that early. I've got to be on the train by seven-thirty." He was very upset and wanted me out of there.

"I'll be up," I said, and wished him good night.

Closing the door behind me, I went on down the hall in puzzlement. What could I have said that annoyed him?

Clean and neat, my own room had fresh linen, along with a china washbowl and matching wash pitcher on a low, granite-topped bureau. By the bed was another small stand with a Bible on it, inscribed GIFT OF THE LADIES' RAILROAD AUXILIARY. Mrs. Ethel Crowe ran a good place indeed, and I would recommend it to anyone. Rachel O'Neal would have likely approved of this place, I thought. But, looking around, it was still a strange room, so different from my own.

I heard a trolley sound over on Granby. Bell clangs and a scrape of steel. Otherwise, there was almost complete silence. The men downstairs had gone to bed and I was sure Mrs. Crowe had donned her nightcap and creamed her face. Breakfast began at six.

I stood a moment longer, realizing it was the first evening I'd ever spent away from the Banks. There was no pound of surf, no cry of night birds. No familiar wand of warmth from Bodie Island Lighthouse. There was a different smell in this room. Nothing like the faint, damp pine odor of my own. Nothing was the same. Everything had changed overnight.

Suddenly I knew why Mike had become upset.

There'd been love and warmth in our house. On those Banks, people cared for each other. I'd told him about something he could never have. No wonder he'd trade Scranton for Heron Head. I thought about him getting cussed and slapped. . . .

In bed, I sighed and twisted around, thinking about Mike and about everything that had happened in the past months. The wreck of the *Malta Empress*. Teetoncey washing ashore, her parents drowning. The whole perplexing business with the silver bullion carried by the *Empress*.

Finally, the night Mama died.

The tears came on without warning.

5

Most of Mrs. Crowe's boarders had already breakfasted and were on their way to the N&W yards with lunch pails, several down to the glistening river to catch a workboat for the Southern Railway terminal over at Pinner's Point, across the way. There was an early morning hurry that I'd never noticed on the Banks, where everyone wriggled stocking toes over a second cup of coffee and mulled the weather before lifting the door latch. There was no calm daybreak here. The city seemed to awaken on the move and was rumbling by seven o'clock.

Mike Grant, standing on the front porch, was leaving, too, for Union Station. Anxious to go. Even fidgety. "Look me up when you come back in, Ben." He seemed wound up.

"I sure will."

The drummer nodded, almost as if I were a stranger, pounded down the steps, and headed rapidly for Main Street, long legs eating ground.

I called after him, "Thanks again."

Floating back came, "Good luck." Then the boy from Scranton, Pennsylvania, turned the corner and was gone. Perhaps forever.

I stayed on the porch a moment longer, then thoughtfully climbed the stairs back to the fourth floor. I usually did not meet someone of a morning and see him go off the next.

I sat on the bed a few minutes and then said to myself, *I've got to do it now. This minute or never.*

Tugging the brown jacket on, adjusting the blue wool cap at an angle on my head, I peered into the small mirror a moment, sticking my chin out, thinking that even a scraggly mustache like Mike Grant's would be of some help. Finally, taking a steadying breath, I descended to the kitchen, where Mrs. Crowe was doing the breakfast dishes. I stood in the doorway. "I'm going now."

She looked up. "Just follow the directions I gave you."

I nodded.

Her eyes took me in, shoes to wool cap. "You should have books in your hand, and be going off to school, not to any rough-and-tumble docks."

I didn't know how to answer that.

She lifted a reddened finger out of steam water and aimed it between my eyes. "If Mr. Jordan is in right mind, he'll tell you to stay exactly put until your big brother comes back."

"Yes, ma'am," I replied, sorely tempted to do just that. "I'll only see what kind of ships they have."

"Be off," she said curtly. "Find out for yourself."

"Yes, ma'am." I nodded and walked out.

It was too early to go to the ship chandlers, I thought—an awful excuse—so I bought a copy of the morning Norfolk *Virginian-Pilot* at the corner of Plume and Granby, then sat down on the curb to read the shipping section, which was always a bible for Filene Midgett. After the mail rider visited, Filene could not make it through the day without reading the arrivals and departures, who was loading what, and what ships were feared lost.

I must go forward a little bit and look back upon that March of 1899. Though I did not realize it and few other people did, it was a time of great change. The twentieth century was nine months away. Electric railways and horseless carriages were already on the streets. Although it was noisy and smelled like something out of the devil's own kitchen, the internal-combustion engine seemed to have a future. Marconi's wireless was soon to be going aboard ships, and the Wright brothers, of Dayton, Ohio, absolutely believed they could do what birds did: fly.

It was all happening and I had little knowledge of it. Even the face of the sea was changing, and I had little knowledge of that either.

That sunny Wednesday, along Norfolk's sprawling waterfront were one hundred and fifteen schooners, one brig, two barkentines, three barks, and forty-eight steamers. They were tucked by wharves and piers all the way from the spines of rail tracks at Lambert's Point south to below the high steel bridge over the Elizabeth River's muddy East Branch.

No sailing man quite believed his day was over, and it wasn't yet, but the British freighter *Inchmaree*, loading for Rotterdam, could carry more in two holds than the biggest schooner in port. According to the newspaper, her manifest (the cargo list) would show 155,174 bushels of corn, 100 bales of cotton, 5,840 sacks of flour, 75 hogsheads of tobacco, 50 barrels of dried apples, 1 flat car of softwood logs, and 67 cars of hardwood logs, and much more. Smoked pork and hog guts and lard.

Along the waterfront, down from Freemason and Jackson and Fayette streets, Commercial Street and the narrow lanes, then flanking the distance of East Main Street, with its saloons and tattoo parlors, there was a sound of winches and a slap of steel cables. The SS *Habil,* West India Fruit and Steamship Company, had loaded general cargo for Kingston, Jamaica. She'd bring back bananas, oranges, and coconuts. The *J. Otterbein* was loading iron pyrites and manure salt for Hamburg. Steamers of the Clyde Line, Merchant & Miners, Johnston Blue Cross, Baltimore Steam Packet, White Star Line to Liverpool, and others, were also working cargo, and mixed in with them were the tall masts of ships that still sailed before the wind.

Almost on the hour, both the iron hulls of the steamers and the bellying canvas of the windjammers passed out Hampton Roads, put Willoughby Spit off to port, and then took departure on Cape Henry, dipping into ocean swell.

I had no thoughts of going to sea on a coal burner. Men of the Banks had always started before the mast and I would be no different.

But that's how it was that Wednesday.

6

AT ABOUT EIGHT O'CLOCK I found myself nervously standing by a brick building near the waterfront, looking at a brass-lettered sign:

J. M. JORDAN'S. SHIP CHANDLERS

ESTABLISHED 1865

It was no will-o'-the-wisp business, by any means. Already the wheels of commerce were grinding in the widening light. Dray wagons were being loaded with ship supplies, and I paused by one wagon as meal, flour, meat; paint, tar, wire, and coils of rope came off pushcarts and out of barrows. A ship would soon sail.

Finally, bracing myself once more, trying to look as tall as possible, hoping my voice wouldn't betray me, I went inside J. M. Jordan's and was immediately awed. Laden shelves climbed right up to the high tin ceiling. Ladders on wheels could reach the very top cans and cartons. There didn't seem to be a thing on earth that wasn't stacked, piled, or barreled somewhere on the premises. If Mr. Burrus thought he had a thriving store in Chicky, he should have taken a gander at Jordan's. There was a selling section, with a long counter; then a wide door and ramp that opened into a bustling warehouse. Toward the back, near an office, was that big coal Heatrola Mrs. Crowe had mentioned. Circled around it, though it wasn't fired this fine spring morning, were the shipmasters, as predicted, talking and smoking and drinking chicory-root coffee from white mugs.

I stood uncertainly looking from face to face,

wondering if any of them knew Reuben. In the blue-coated flesh, they were a sight to see. Weathered and muttonchopped and full-white-bearded and clean-shaven, they were nothing less than bedazzling. Kings of the ocean. If any of them were coasting captains, masters who made short hauls along the coast, they couldn't help but know the *Elnora Langhans*, because she'd sailed the Atlantic shores and down in the Caribbean for many years.

Listening to them a moment, I decided to approach a counter clerk and ask forthrightly for Mr. Jordan. Meanwhile, my eyes caught several large blackboards on the back wall. SHIPS IN PORT, well more than a hundred of them, were chalked in; SHIPS OVERDUE & UNREPORTED, three of them. Closer to the boards, I recognized a few names I'd seen before through the long glass from the cupola at Heron Head Station, ships that had passed close inshore. Date of arrival and scheduled date of departure were by each in-port ship, along with the lying-to wharf or anchorage.

Still delaying, I read the name of each vessel

and then forced myself to the counter. "Could I please see Mr. Jordan?"

The clerk was gray-haired, aproned, and not friendly. "About what, boy?"

"A job."

"Mr. Robert Keen does the hiring. He's in the warehouse."

"I mean a job on a ship. Mrs. Crowe sent me and I think Mr. Jordan knows my brother, mate on the *Elnora Langhans*."

"Wait here." The clerk seemed harried for so early in the morning.

In a moment, a portly, kindly faced man filled the office doorway, heavy gold watch chain taut across his sloping vest. "Mrs. Crowe sent you? Why, I thought she hated anything to do with ships."

The captains laughed.

I began walking toward the chandler.

"For what did she send you?"

"I'm trying to find a cabin boy's job. On a sailing ship bound for the Caribbean. Any ship. Reuben's down there somewhere and I—" The words were escaping all too fast, I knew.

"Slow down. For one thing, very few sailing vessels take on boys nowadays, more trouble than they're worth. For another thing, who are you? Who's Reuben?"

"I'm Ben O'Neal. Reuben's my brother. We're from Heron Head, on the Hatteras Banks. Mama died last month and I've got to find—"

"Slow down, Ben."

"Yessir."

I licked my lips and started off again. "Reuben's on the *Elnora Langhans,* on a run to the Barbadoes and Trinidad from Port Fernandino and I want to see him. Very badly. I must see him."

Mr. Jordan nodded understandingly. "I know Reuben. Fine man. But you don't look much like him."

"No, sir." (Reuben resembled Mama, with a big nose and reddish-brown hair. I looked like John O'Neal, with dark hair and a smaller nose.)

"I also knew your papa," Mr. Jordan went on. "But I doubt either one of them would want me to send you helter-skelter down to the Caribbean. No guarantee you'll get within two hundred miles of the *Langhans.* She may be coming north when you're going south. And I don't know offhand of any ship that needs a boy." He looked over to the collection of masters around his cold stove.

A captain with a heavy, round, crimson face and white muttonchops answered. "I don't need one. I'm headed for Boston, anyway."

"Sorry," replied another, and it was echoed by a third.

A fourth said, "Last boy I had stumbled all over himself and was seasick the whole voyage."

I turned my head. "I won't be seasick."

There was skeptical laughter.

Feeling everything slipping away from me, I looked back at Mr. Jordan. "But I came up here to go to sea . . ."

"I think you should go back home."

Desperation fell over me and I said frantically, "There's no one at home. I have to find Reuben." It was imperative after last night's long think.

Mr. Jordan sighed and looked over the in-port board, studying it at length. The captains examined it, too. "There's only one vessel leaving for the Caribbean the rest of the week," Mr. Jordan finally said. "Sails to Barbados day after tomorrow. But I wouldn't recommend it to a dock rat."

The master with the muttonchops added, "I would just as soon sail with a combination of dodo bird and hangman as I would with Josiah Reddy."

Josiah Reddy. The name meant nothing to me.

"Aw, Sam," said another captain. "You're just jealous. Joe Reddy's a bit odd, but he's got the finest, fastest bark on this coast. He beats us all in and out of port."

"Dodo bird," repeated Mr. Jordan, as though he had a bitter memory.

Cap'n Sam laughed hollowly. "Odd? He still uses sea chanteys when he gets under way. Won't hoist sail with the donkey engine. Makes his men pull every inch up. He's been known to sit out on his jibboom and sing to the ocean. He sprinkles sugar on the water to rise a breeze."

"First-class lunatic," said Mr. Jordan.

Everyone laughed again.

"And something else. That bosun of his . . ."

added Mr. Jordan, leaving the description dangling ominously.

"Gebbert? He's mean and rough and slave-drivin', but he gets the work done. I'd like to have him in my ship."

I didn't flinch through all this. There wasn't a more difficult man anywhere than Hardie Miller, of Kinnakeet, and I had survived him on more than one occasion.

Mr. Jordan continued. "Ben, tell you what, since you seem so bound and determined, in about a month, young Cap'n Ted Hubbard will put in with the *Omar Hubbard,* of the Columbus Line. I'll make sure you get passage. He goes to Kingston, Barbados, Trinidad, and other places. You'll likely have to work your way, but you'll be in good, sane hands. Reuben knows him, I'm sure."

I shook my head. "I can't wait a month, sir. I haven't got that much money."

Mr. Jordan rubbed his jaw. "Well, I guess we can find something for you to do around here. Shine brass or empty spittoons. Sweep up. Two dollars and lunch a week. Now, you go back to Mrs. Crowe's and then report here tomorrow morning at seven-thirty."

"Isn't there any other sailing ship leaving this week or next?" I asked, feeling low.

"I'm afraid not," he answered. "You got here too late for the *Lois Solomon,* and the *Cashamara* sails Monday but she's a British steamer."

As he turned back into the office and the captains began chatting again, I lingered on to look at the in-port board. The masters weren't listed. Only the names of the vessels. Which one did Cap'n Reddy command?

Just as I was leaving, very depressed, Mr. Jordan came back out of the office and called to me. "Ben, I almost forgot. There's a message here for you."

I could not believe it. No one but Mrs. Crowe and the railroaders knew that I'd come to Jordan's. I took it anyway and glanced at the handwriting on the envelope. My disbelief turned to astonishment. Unless I was very mistaken, the penmanship, neat and orderly, was done by none other than a thistle-waisted four-foot-ten-inch girl I knew as Teetoncey. Built like a healthy broomstraw and sharp-nosed, at this moment she was supposed to be in, or nearing, London, her home. At least those were the intentions of not two weeks before.

I thanked the ship chandler and stuffed the envelope into my hip pocket, refusing to open it; fearful of opening it. Though I was alternately smitten and peeved with her, every time I'd been involved with that girl disaster seemed to lurk.

Outside, another dray was being loaded, and I stepped up to one of the handlers. "Excuse me, could you please tell me which ship Cap'n Josiah Reddy commands?"

The burly man finished shoving a barrel of salted fish into the wagon bed, wiped sweat from his brow, rubbed his hands on his dirty apron, then laughed. "No trouble tellin' you that. He commands the bitch of the Atlantic."

The coarse language was startling. "Could I please have her name?"

"The *Christine Conyers*, prettiest four-masted

backbreaker from Cape Race to the Horn, so they say."

Backbreaker? Nonetheless I asked, "Where is she?"

"Don't rightly know. But you can find out at Hudgins & Hurst, chandlers and sailmakers, No. 11 Roanoke Dock. They provision her. We don't. They're reservin' a place for Joe Reddy in the insane asylum up to Richmond."

Everyone thought that Mis' Mehaly Blodgett, of Buxton Woods, was loonier than a feeble-minded pelican, but she wasn't once you got to know her.

I thanked him.

"What's your interest in the *Conyers*?"

"I hope to hire on as cabin boy. To the Barbadoes." There was only one of those islands, but everybody on the Banks spelled it and pronounced it that way, as if it were two.

The handler laughed caustically. "You'd be better off swimmin' there." He went about his work.

On that note, I left the area of Jordan's and

went around the corner. I stopped and put my back up against a brick wall and fished the envelope out of my pocket. It was addressed: *Ben O'Neal, of Heron Head, Hatteras Banks. Urgent.*

I debated a moment, then ripped it open. It was from the girl, all right, and someone else.

It said:

Dearest Ben:
I am on Phillips's Barge No. 7, tied up south of the Clyde Line docks. Come quick. I need your help.

It was signed, "Love, T. & B. D." I read it twice.

Unmistakably, Teetoncey and that troublesome dog, Boo. They weren't anywhere near London.

It seemed to me that I had enough peril and difficulties ahead without further calamity arising. Why it was, I don't know, but I had the feeling that message was going to hang around my neck like an anchor chain.

7

I FELT NEED for a good stiffener, as Mr. Burrus would say before having a root beer. And some hard thought, additionally. Being near Robert Holmes, Druggist, I went on in there and sat down at that solid-onyx Tuff Revier double-stand soda-water fountain, one of the most beautiful things I'd ever seen. I ordered a lemon drink. Then I began to think, first things first. No matter Teetoncey's plight, whatever it happened to be, I had to get to the *Christine Conyers* and apply for a job. Sailing day after tomorrow, there was no time to waste. That was all settled.

What I couldn't understand was why Tee wasn't on the *Vulcania,* or a similar steamship, about to make landfall in England. She had left the Banks eight days before and from my information was to be shipped immediately by Consul Calderham to New York, thence to London to resume living in her big and fancy house. Even though her parents were dead, courtesy of the sea, and she'd have to live with the servants now, bossing them around, there was not much to pity about that girl. She had pluck. We had gone through a whole big good-bye scene, professing admiration for each other; I had watched the *Neuse* sail away with her, accompanied by my former duck dog, a departure gift. They had taken to each other. Now she was still around. And with her, roughly a hundred pounds of yellow-gold Labrador, with soulful dark eyes and overlong ears, the most one-minded dog on earth. Worthless now that he had retired from retrieving ducks.

I could only imagine that she had foolishly run away from the uncaring British consul for one reason or another, not that I could blame her. Yet she was duty-bound to return to London and resume her wealthy life in Belgravia, one of the better sections of that city.

For a moment, I thought about going directly to Phillips's Barge No. 7 to determine what she had done, right or wrong, but then decided to visit Consul Calderham first. Tee was not above twisting the truth, as I had learned, and, perhaps, neither was Calderham. But it seemed sensible to get his story before confronting the girl.

Meanwhile, I finished the lemon drink, much refreshed, and went along to Hudgins & Hurst, at No. 11 Roanoke Dock.

On the way, I saw my first automobile, and not the steam variety, parked in front of a dry-goods store. A slew of people, at least fifty, were around it. A two-seated gasoline Winton, with a buggy roof and steering tiller, carbide lights, it made me hold my breath. A boy in a long gray coat, wearing goggles carelessly over his cap brim, was polishing it. One waspish man said, "I'd rather have a Haynes-Apperson." Why, I would have given anything just to sit in either one and would like to have stayed there all day. But after a half hour of watching, I forced myself onward.

A little later, I navigated by a warehouse below Front Street and walked out onto the wharfage, and there sat the *Christine Conyers*.

I gasped. She literally shone in the midmorning sun. A big square-rigger, deeply laden, black of hull with white trim, she was the most outstanding sailing vessel I'd ever seen. The brass on her glittered; the decks were like Mama's sink top, scrubbed to whiteness. No vessel had ever been spat upon and polished any more than the *Conyers*.

How could they possibly make fun of Captain Josiah Reddy when he commanded such a ship? Jealousy, as one master had said, was likely the reason. I stood quite a while just looking at her, angel figurehead on her bow to the fancy gold-inscribed name on her stern, four masts stretching up to the cloudless sky.

Finally I summoned up all my courage and

strode down the dock beside her, reaching the gangway. There were a few men working on deck, notably one hulking man standing with his hands on his hips, and I guessed that he was the bosun, Gebbert. Boss of the deck crew.

I said to him, "Permission to come aboard, sir?"

He turned. He had small eyes, usually the mark of a mean man, and a face that should have been slaughtered with last fall's hogs, above a short neck. His hands and arms were huge, shoulders thick and wide. I think Filene would have had trouble besting this bosun, though Prochorus Midgett, who was not above using his feet, might have handled him.

I will try to spell it the way he talked it: "Vat do you vant?" he asked, chickpea eyes hard as whetstone.

"I'd like to apply for a cabin boy's job," I said, determined not to let his looks sway me.

"Vee don't need no boys on das ship," he replied.

"I'll work for my keep," I said. "I need passage

to the Barbadoes. I'll do anything just for my food and the voyage."

The other men had stopped work and were looking at me. Over the bosun's shoulder, one tall, owl-eyed sailor shook his head as if to tell me, *Stay on the dock.*

"Vee don't need no boys on das ship," the bosun repeated in a growing growl. Surfman Mark Jennette once told me that a good bosun had marlinspikes for fingers, hair like hemp rope, and Stockholm tar for blood. This man had all three, I did believe.

Just then, another man, a rather small, trim man, stepped around the outboard side of the afterhouse and took a summing-up look at me. Hair turning ivory, but dark-browed, he was dressed in a business suit, had on a red tie and high celluloid collar. With a bulldoggy, weather-lined face, deep-set gray eyes, he stared at me piercingly but spoke instead to the bosun. "Hans, how many times have I told you to be courteous." For such a small man, he had a deep, lilting voice.

That was my introduction to the infamous

Captain Josiah Reddy, of Port Wilmington, Delaware.

The bosun said, "I thought vee vere going to hire a man for dat job."

The captain ignored him and moved across the deck to stand by the polished rail. "Show me your hands," he said.

He should have looked at my knees; they were dancing. I held my hands out.

"Palms up."

I turned them over. They shook a bit.

"You've done some work," said Cap'n Reddy. Those dark eyebrows, coarse as horse bristle, stood out like caterpillars beneath his yellow-white hair.

"Yessir," I managed, after a swallow.

"Do you like music?" he asked, voice coming up from his shoes.

I could take it or leave it alone, but I gambled. "Yessir."

"Do you like Siamese cats?"

I gambled again. "Very much." I didn't like cats of any kind.

He nodded. "Be in front of Hudgins & Hurst

tomorrow at eight o'clock. Parley Bakerby is my shipping master. Tell him to sign you on as steward's boy at a dollar a week."

I almost collapsed, both from joy and fright. But I gave him a snappy, "Yessir," having no idea what a steward's boy did, and not caring. With that, and no more words, he walked rapidly toward the afterhouse.

Defeated, the bosun stood glowering at me, and behind his back the thin sailor who had cast me a warning head-shake was now circling his finger around his temple. That gesture, I think, was to tell me that the bosun was insane. Perhaps the captain. Maybe both. Or the gesture might have been directed at me.

I got away from there as fast as I could, nonetheless pleased that I had obtained employment, still determined not to let false impressions of the bosun and the *Conyers*'s master interrupt my plans. I had come to Norfolk to go to sea, and that was almost accomplished.

8

MIND WHIRLING AROUND happily, success within reach, I went straightaway to Mrs. Crowe's, there to announce I'd found a ship. She answered crisply, "The N&W machine shop will still be here when your ship is long sunk," which tended to dampen my enthusiasm. But, with one problem solved, I asked Mrs. Crowe how I might find the British consul.

"You going to England?"

"No," I said, but then had to tell the whole story of Tee again, and I was truthfully beginning to sound like a wax record. How she'd been flung up on our beach after the *Malta Empress* wrecked; how Mama and I had nursed her back to sanity; how Consul Calderham had tried to spirit her away; how she'd caused a commotion with her family's silver treasure on Heron bar; how I'd finally shipped her north less than ten days ago, and now like a scuppernong vine she was still around me. Mrs. Crowe blinked quite a lot through the whole thing but then went to her writing desk and pulled out a paperbound book entitled Norfolk City Directory.

I looked over her shoulder. At the top and bottom of each page were advertisements for everything from Tom's Creek Coal to Quattlebaum's Pharmacy. She found the British consulate on Magazine Lane, north from 59 Queen Street. That book was a storehouse of local information.

It was now about noontime and she served me lunch, though that wasn't in our contract, and I spent another hour, simply to pass it, just looking over the city directory. In it was everything from Eastwood's Detective Agency, on Yaxley Lane, to the Great Atlantic & Pacific Tea Company and the La Mode Hair Dressing Parlor for Fashionable Ladies. An interesting document. Then I went along to Magazine Lane to renew acquaintance with Consul Calderham.

No sooner had I knocked on his door and opened it when he rose up from behind his cluttered desk, seemingly surprised. In the background was a British flag and a silver-framed picture I took to be the Queen of England. She was old and kindly looking.

He shouted, "You!"

I was taken aback. I had done nothing. So far.

"I might have known," he yelled, face all balled up. His right hand was swathed in bandages. His derby hat was off, and I found out that he'd been concealing baldness from me. He'd always worn his hat when he visited the Banks to spirit Tee away. Unsuccessfully, I might add.

"Where is that atrocious girl?" he continued in a shouting voice.

I answered respectfully, being careful not to lie, staying the good Methodist, "Isn't she on her way to London?"

"You know full well she isn't."

I did know that but believed it best to draw him out. "You mean she didn't get on the *Vulcania*?"

It's a wonder his shining head didn't turn cherry red. He yelled, "She ran away a week ago last night, along with that flea-bitten dog."

Boo did have a lot of fleas. "Why did she do that?"

"Because she's incorrigible! She's a disgrace to the Crown."

That was not my picture of Tee. She'd disrupted our lives on the Banks without meaning to. But, generally, she'd seemed to be a kind and caring girl. Or so I thought. I said, "I'm sorry to hear that."

Then he simmered down a minute and asked, suspiciously, "Why are you here? All this trouble can be traced directly to you and that idiotic lighthouse keeper."

That was only partially true, and Filene wasn't a lighthouse keeper. He happened to be one of the best surf captains on any coast. I tried to remain calm. "I came here to go to sea," I replied honestly. "I just dropped by to inquire about Teetoncey's departure."

"Above all, her name isn't Teetoncey. It is Wendy Lynn Appleton, a British subject."

"I know, sir," I said, careful to be polite.

"And I hope she's been burned at the stake by now. She's not only a runaway, she's a thief."

I couldn't believe that. I said, in Tee's behalf, quoting Mrs. Crowe from another conversation, "She's as honest as a creek pebble."

Calderham's reply smoldered. "She'll soon turn honest when she's arrested. I have the local authorities out looking for her."

"The police?" I asked, startled.

"The police," he said, firmly.

"There must be some mistake, Mr. Calderham. Tee's a fine girl . . ."

Suddenly he was turning livid once more and waved that bandaged hand at me threateningly. "I've a good mind to call the authorities again and have you arrested."

Now I decided to stand my ground. He'd

bullied us enough at Heron Head. "I've done nothing wrong."

"I can think of twenty things," he responded. "I've a good idea that you and that chinless man tried to kill me. I almost drowned in that open boat." He was referring to Jabez Tillett and a trip they took down Pamlico Sound in December. It had been cold and rough. But almost getting pneumonia as a result was an act of God, not ordained by Jabez or myself.

I said, defensively, "There is not a better sailor around than Jabez Tillett."

The consul hit his swollen, bandaged hand on the desk edge and screamed in pain, and I thought it best to leave, having learned not much.

Taking my time, stalling the rendezvous with the girl, I went to Commercial Street down by the ferry landing and watched the paddle wheelers come in for a while, making positively bad landings against the high pilings, just smashing into them, and then walked along the N&W tracks, which are in the middle of Water Street, until I saw the Clyde Line docks down by the river. I turned and went to them, then began strolling along the Eastern Branch of the Elizabeth, looking at various ships, trying to keep my mind off Tee as one tries to avoid a toothache.

Soon the Clyde Line slips ended and I began to see many barges tied up along the wharf frontage. Some were singles; others were tied in tandem. A few belonged to the F. S. Royster Company; some to Virginia Iron, Coal and Coke. Then I saw Phillips's barges, and down toward where Newton Creek dumped into the river was No. 7, properly named the *Rock Thompson*, of Tappahannock, Virginia.

It was an old beat-up barge and looked as though it might have been hauling stone of some type. There was a cabin on the after end, a wooden house that went from side to side, about fifteen feet wide, with a stove stack sticking up. Gulls perched sassily on a laundry line, messing up the deck below instead of helping needy soil. (Bargemasters live in the cabins as the boxy boats are towed up and down the rivers, up Chesapeake Bay, down the inland canals.) Except for a thin curl of smoke coming up the stack, No. 7 appeared to be out of service. I checked up and down the dock for spying eyes, then quickly clambered aboard and knocked on the cabin door. I also whispered, "Teetoncey."

The door opened a crack, and in the gloom I could see four eyes. Two were about eight inches below my level of sight; the other two were about thigh-high from the deck. Then a voice said, "Ben?"

I sighed. "Who else?"

The door opened and Tee flung her arms around my neck. Deciding to find out what it was all about before I made a decision, I stood a little rigid and aloof, but even Boo Dog seemed pleased to see me. Jumping up, licking my cheek. So there I was, the British castaway girl around my neck and the gold dog pushing up against me. Worried that we'd be seen, I said, "Let's get inside."

Inside was like a dungeon and stunk pretty bad from its former occupant, but as soon as I could adjust my vision, I saw that Teetoncey'd completely settled in, with blankets, a couple of pots, and some food. She had spunk, all right, living alone there.

She said, "Oh, Ben, I knew you'd come. Let me look at you."

I hadn't changed much physically in eight days. "What are you doing here?" I asked. "You're supposed to be in London today or tomorrow." That *Vulcania*, I knew, could cross in less than six days.

"You don't know what I've been through," she said.

Well, I'd gone through a few things myself.

Boo Dog sat down in his usual position by her feet, looking up, tongue out, wearing that silly grin I knew so well.

"What have you been through?" I asked.

Tee went over and sat down at the bargemaster's battered table, and I sat down across from her, after opening a dingy burlap curtain to let some light in. She didn't look as if she'd been ground up by Calderham; she hadn't lost an ounce of weight, which she could ill afford to lose. Still pretty as ever; afternoon sunlight caught in her daisy hair, turned her eyes July blue.

"The consul met me, as planned, and was very kind and polite. He helped me shop a bit in the afternoon and I was to take the train north the following morning, then sail from New York. All went well until he lit up his cigar after dinner. Then he said to me, 'You cannot take that dog with you, Miss Appleton.'"

I knew it. I knew it. I knew it. I looked over at Boo and could have cheerfully punched his pinkish bulb nose. If ever a hound was wreaking havoc on earth, he was. To Boo, I said, "Damn all, you caused it."

Tee said indignantly, "Don't blame it on him."

I shook my head in disgust. All this would have to happen on the eve of my departure. "What happened then?"

"I asked why not. The consul said he didn't want to make animal arrangements with the Cunard Line. It was beneath his dignity. Besides, he said he jolly well did not want Boo to contaminate the breed in England. And I jolly well told him what I thought of him."

Contaminate the breed? That got to me swiftly. "Boo is one of the finest dogs in this country." The nerve of the consul.

"Yes, he is," said Tee. "And I insisted that Boo must go wherever I went, but the consul was equally insistent that Boo would go back to the 'miserable' Outer Banks, where he belonged."

Oh, that consul was an obstinate, unfeeling man. "Then what happened?"

"We had a fight."

"A regular fight?"

"Well, not quite. The consul got up out of his chair, came close, and shook his fist at me. Boo promptly bit it."

Calderham's bandaged hand! I had to laugh. I knew there was something about that dog that I liked and went over and congratulated him, then sat down again.

Tee smiled at me. "So here I am."

"Yes," I said, wondering what to do about it. "You know, the police are looking for you."

"I thought they were," said Tee, seemingly not disturbed. "They were snooping around here day before yesterday. Ben, I think that consul is determined to get me to England. I think he's obsessed."

I said, "So do I. But you've done a foolish thing, Tee. Maybe you should give yourself up. I can find some way to send Boo home."

Tee tried some womanly wile on me precisely at that point. She said, "Ben, let's go back to the Banks. We belong together."

I sat upright. "We've been through that before. We cannot live together in that house, and that's that. I'll say it again, there's no preacher who'll marry two young'uns together." I was very firm and her face drooped a little. I realized she'd been plotting for days. Something else suddenly occurred to me. "How did you find me?"

"I simply left the same note at Jordan's, Oscar Smith's, D. S. Baum, and Hudgins & Hurst. You said you'd be going to all the best ship chandlers."

That girl was not unintelligent. "All right, you found me. But now we have to figure a way out of this."

"Why can't I just come with you, wherever you're going? I've got no schedule to make." She pronounced it *shed-yule*, as always, British style.

"That is absolutely impossible," I replied emphatically. "Not four hours ago I was hired as a seaman aboard the finest ship on the coast, the four-master bark *Christine Conyers*." I was very proud of that. "What's more," I continued, "we're sailing day after tomorrow to the Barbadoes."

She said quickly, "It's not *the Barbadoes*. It's simply Barbados, and the port is Bridgetown."

"Well, that's the way we say it on the Banks—*the Barbadoes*—and I know that the port is Bridgetown. Reuben goes in and out there all the time, and that's who I'm going to meet."

"You know nothing about Barbados and Bridgetown," she said. "You've never even been there. I have."

"I'll find out for myself," I replied, dedicated to do just that.

"So you'll just leave us here alone?" she said gloomily. "You'll abandon us? That isn't like you, Ben."

Weariness rather than gloom was in my voice when I answered. "Tee, I'm going to get you both off this barge and on your way to New York, I hope."

She turned chilly toward me. "I can take care of myself."

I met that challenge. "Well, why did you *urgently* send me a message?"

She turned sullen-silent, and after a moment of thought I said, "I'll try to get you into my boardinghouse overnight. The landlady doesn't like female boarders but—"

Tee interrupted. "Why doesn't she like female boarders?"

I had to be honest. "Because they hang their bloomers out the window."

Tee snapped, "I've never hung my underwear out of any window."

That was her business. I shrugged but happened to glance over at Boo. As an afterthought, I said, "She doesn't permit pets, either."

Tee was seething by now. "Ben, why don't you leave the barge. We can take care of ourselves."

I sighed once more, feeling burdened. "Tee, I'll help all I can. Mama would want me to do it, I know. And I want to do it."

Looking down her sharp nose at me, she said, "Thank you," so British.

I got up and started gathering her blankets and pots. "Where did you get these?" I asked.

"I took them from the consulate, along with thirty-one dollars."

I almost dropped them. So that's why Calderham had accused her of being a thief.

"Oh, don't look so shocked," Tee said. "The British Government has been taking our taxes for years and never gives a tuppence back."

You know, she was right. The U.S. Government does the same thing.

We went along to Mrs. Crowe's, Tee trailing Boo and myself by about a half block to avoid suspicions. Undoubtedly, the Norfolk police were looking for a blond girl and a gold dog. I had her wear my blue cap.

9

BEFORE SUPPER, one railroader, not a Carolina man, wanted to know why I called that girl *Tee-toncey*. Simple, I explained. It was a Banks word that meant teeny-tiny, and that seemed to satisfy him. One look at her and he could see that the name fitted the orphan like a toenail.

Then, while we ate, Tee told her story of the past months, losing her parents in the shipwreck, etc., gaining a lot of sympathy for herself and Boo. She did well, and didn't exaggerate too much. When she came to the part about Consul Calderham waving a fist at her, Mr. Stone angrily rose half out of his chair and began muttering about going to Magazine Lane and breaking the consul's jaw.

Mrs. Crowe said her piece: "Sit down, and be quiet, Mr. Stone."

I had told them all about finding employment on the *Christine Conyers,* but they didn't seem to be much interested in it now. Teetoncey was the center of all attention, with her Thames River accent, and I turned silent. When she talked about her previous life in London, and living in the Belgravia house, with a cook and gardener and tweeny maids, Mrs. Crowe half laughed and said, "Wouldn't you like to have a nice foster mother?" I believe she was far more serious than she appeared to be.

Tee wisely did not tell them about Calderham's notifying the authorities, and throughout all this, Boo was down in the blackness of the cellar, surrounded by jars of pickles and beets and strings of onions, moaning now and then. He was very unhappy down there, having always had the run of any house on the Banks that he happened to visit. But Mrs. Crowe, though readily accepting

Tee after I'd explained her plight, was very firm about the hound.

After supper, Mrs. Crowe let the dirty dishes stay where they sat, and we all went into the parlor to talk about getting Tee to London without the assistance of Consul Calderham. It was certain he'd find a way to undo the dog. The bite on the hand, though well deserved, had probably sealed Boo's fate.

It was Mrs. Crowe who said to Tee, "Well, as long as you have your credentials, there's no reason for you not to get on a train and go straight to New York, find yourself a ship to London, and be on your way." There was a couthy woman if I'd ever heard one.

When the castaway girl had "taken" the blankets and pots, plus the "tax rebate" of thirty-one dollars from Calderham's desk drawer, she had also lifted her Cunard Line ticket and other credentials for the Transatlantic crossing. So, actually, she was ready to travel.

One of the railroad men, named J. H. Riddleberger, who worked for the N&W in the passenger division, said, "She can get out of here early in the morning on a Little Pennsy ferry to Cape Charles, then take the NYP&N up to Philly, transfer on to New York City—"

He sounded very knowledgeable, but I asked, "What is all that, sir?"

"Well," he explained, "the Little Pennsy— New York, Philadelphia, and Norfolk Railroad— starts at Cape Charles, on the Virginia Peninsula, then the train goes north to Philadelphia, where it joins the Big Pennsy tracks that go everywhere. There's a well-run ferry from here to Cape Charles."

That was a most important conference there in Mrs. Crowe's parlor amid the ferns, and the scheduling sounded good.

"Will they accept Boo Dog?" Tee immediately wanted to know.

"Gladly," said Mr. Riddleberger. "You just tie him up with a bowl of water in the baggage car. He'll enjoy the ride."

That dog was unbelievably lucky.

So it was all settled. Tee would take the NYP&N ferry, which docked between the C&O slips and the Old Bay Line, walking distance, at

6 A.M. and be off to New York and London without the help of Consul Calderham and freed of the Norfolk police dragnet.

A moment later, Boo let out one of those long, mournful cries from the basement, one of those graveyard caterwauls that a hound is capable of, and I went down there while Tee assisted Mrs. Crowe with the supper dishes.

Soon the British girl joined me under the single Edison lightbulb, a fascinating thing, that hung from the ceiling near the furnace, and we talked for a long time, Boo contentedly at her feet, enjoying strokes of her hand along his head and ears. There was no question that they were inseparable now. Calderham could have just as soon split the Rock of Gibraltar as split those two.

But just to discourage Tee from any thoughts of following me to sea, I told her the truth about Cap'n Reddy and the bosun: that I'd heard from reliable sources that Reddy was insane and the bosun a bucko hangman; that the *Conyers* was actually a hellship. She seemed to understand that it was simply a very risky means to get me in touch with Reuben. I also had the strong notion she'd make a last-ditch effort to snare me, persuade me to take her back to Heron Head and there "live happily ever after." But, apparently, she was now resigned to making the inevitable voyage home. She even talked about things she'd do right away in the Belgravia house, and it was one of the most pleasant conversations we'd ever had.

About nine, Mrs. Crowe stuck her head down the steps and suggested we get some sleep. Tee would have to be awakened at five, and of course, I had to be on Roanoke Dock, with my seabag, at eight.

Having been pampered for more than an hour, Boo was sufficiently sleepy now, so off we went to our respective rooms, the day having ended successfully for all.

However, a few minutes after 5 A.M., Mrs. Crowe entered my room to awaken me with shattering news. "She's gone!"

"Oh, no," I said. Another of W. L. Appleton's surprises.

"I went in to wake her up, and she's nowhere in the house. Neither is that dog."

I couldn't believe it. Gone to where? It didn't seem likely that Calderham and the police could have located her and spirited her off. Had she run off again, and why?

The answer soon emerged. We found two notes on the dining-room table. One was to Mrs. Crowe:

Dear Mrs. Crowe:
I can never thank you enough for allowing us to stay in your lovely home. And please extend my gratitude to the railroad men for their sound advice. I am on my way.

Sincerely,
Wendy Lynn Appleton

"Such a sweet girl," said Mrs. Crowe.
"Yes," I replied, but uncertainly.
Then I opened my note:

Dearest Ben:
I could not bear the thought of us saying good-bye so decided to go to the ferry alone with Boo. Please don't follow us. I prefer to think of the

good times, not the sad times. Do write to me,
and I shall write to you.

Love,

Teetoncey

Despite myself, I had a lump in my throat. I then agreed, "A very sweet girl."

Since she was already up, Mrs. Crowe decided to fix breakfast, and I ate, with not much appetite, at about a quarter to six. My thoughts were of Tee. Then, about six, I went up to the fourth-floor landing to watch the NYP&N ferry pull away. It was too far off and dawn-lit to make out the girl with the daisy hair and the gold-coated dog, but I waved watery-eyed, as the vessel backed into the channel, blew its sorrowful whistle, and began to step out for Cape Charles.

Though it should have been a happy morning in my life, I felt somewhat depressed as I packed everything into my seabag and began the wait until seven-thirty to go to Hudgins & Hurst to meet the shipping master. I fiddled around for a while, went out on the front porch and rocked for a while, said good-bye to all the railroaders as they left for the day, and watched the big clock in the parlor.

Finally, just before seven-thirty, I went in to Mrs. Crowe to bid her farewell, wonderful woman that she was. She softened a bit and told me to take care of myself, be certain to come back to her establishment, then happened to ask the name of the shipping master.

"Parley Bakerby," I said.

Her face got as red as her hair. "Do you know who he is?"

"No," I admitted.

"He owns the Tidewater Saloon. He's a scoundrel. Offers the men loans of ten dollars when he signs them on, just so they'll come back to his den of sin when they pay off at voyage's end."

"I didn't know that," I said. "I won't ask for a loan."

"You be careful," Mrs. Crowe said.

I promised I would, shook her hand, and departed.

10

ON ARRIVAL, there was already a group of scruffy men hanging around Roanoke Dock, and I stayed strictly away from them, trying to make as if I were just sightseeing around. Several sailors appeared to be tipsy, even at this early hour; several others appeared to have the shakes, which I had myself but not from any night in the saloons.

In about ten minutes, Parley Bakerby came puffing along, a lot of official papers in his hands. He was a pink-faced, potbellied man with silky hair and tiny red veins on his nose and cheeks, looking just like a politician and similar destructive persons. He went inside Hudgins & Hurst, towed a small table outside, and sat down heavily behind it, saying in a hoarse voice, "*Conyers* voyage, boys, come an' sign your papers."

Everyone lined up, me at the end. To the first man, who wore a sweater and checkered cloth cap, he said, "Nils, why you tryin' to read 'em? Just sign 'em. You know you can't read a line."

"Where we goin' this time, an' with what?" Nils asked Parley.

"Barbados, a little general cargo; then on to Rio, thousands o' barrels o' flour. Bring coffee home. Pay off north o' Cape Hatteras. Twelve a month."

Nils took the pen and signed while Parley said, "You know the routine. Throw your gear in that wagon over there an' jus' wait. You need any money this trip, Nils?"

Ah, hah, I thought: the loan.

Nils shook his head and Parley said, "Well, come by an' see your ol' friend when you get back. I'll buy you a whiskey."

Nils walked to the wagon.

The second man looked very old.

"Who are you?" the saloonkeeper asked.

"Mumford."

Parley demanded, "Open your mouth, Mumford."

There wasn't a tooth in it. Parley squinted at the sailor. "How old are you?"

"Fifty-seven."

Parley grunted. "Poppycock. You been fifty-seven for twenty years. *Conyers* can't use you."

The old man's shoulders slumped and he shuffled off. I felt sorry for him.

It went that way through thirteen or fourteen more men, Parley Bakerby hiring three-quarters of them. Then, suddenly, I was at the table looking down at that nose with little, leafy red lines in it.

"Why are you here?" the shipping master asked.

I replied, "Cap'n Reddy said to sign me on as steward's boy. Dollar a week."

Parley Bakerby laughed. That's all. He made no other comment but looked at me closely as he shoved the articles toward me, pushing out the pen at the same time.

I did not get beyond the first paragraph when Bakerby said gruffly, "Boy, don't read it, just sign it. I ain't got all day."

I did as directed.

Then he shoved another paper across, and I filled that in.

While he was filling in his section, I looked at another piece of U.S. Government paper displayed on that table:

SCALE OF PROVISIONS TO BE ALLOWED AND SERVED OUT TO CREW DURING VOYAGE

Water . . . . 5 qts. daily
Biscuit . . . . ½ lb daily
Beef, salt . . . . 3¾ lb weekly
Pork, salt . . . . 3 lb weekly
Flour . . . . 1½ lb weekly
Potatoes . . . . 7 lb weekly

Bakerby's voice jarred my thoughts as it occurred to me that we'd be eating a lot of potatoes. "Throw your bag in that wagon," he said. There was no good-bye, good luck, or offer of a loan.

By the time I picked up my seabag, he was already towing the table back into Hudgins & Hurst and I was an official crew member of the *Christine Conyers*. There was nothing special about any part of it.

Soon, along with the rest, I was walking behind the double-horse wagon, about to start my long-awaited career. After a half block of plodding, with us looking like pallbearers behind a load of canvas sacks, I maneuvered up beside Nils, who was grizzled and hunch-shouldered, with a square face and hooky nose. I told him about the skinny sailor who'd warned me not to come aboard the *Conyers*.

Nils said back, "There are one or three or more of them on every ship. They ain't happy 'less they mumble 'bout food an' the work an' the cap'n an' the bosun an' the cockroaches. They ain't happy till they make everybody else unhappy. They're mostly mouth an' ain't worth a damn themselves. Sea lawyers, they're called, worse than the land kind."

So much for that. "Is the captain really crazy?"

He looked down and over to reply. "Yes an' no," with a chuckle added.

"Does he throw sugar into the sea to rise a breeze?"

"Yep. That don't make him crazy."

"He sing from the bowsprit?"

"Sometimes."

I said, "He asked whether I like music and cats."

Nils laughed. "He owns a mangy cat an' plays the pump organ an' shoots at waterspouts."

He sounded crazy to me. "They don't like him at Jordan's."

Nils laughed and laughed. "That was in his drinkin' an' gamblin' days. He used to beat Jordan at five-card stud, and once Jordan was slow payin' up. So Joe Reddy hired a horse an' galloped in there an' shot up the molasses jugs. They had a helluva time moppin' that stuff up."

"I've never heard of a cap'n like him," I said.

Nils replied, "He's slowed down now, but ain't above usin' his fists if you git uppity."

"Why do you sail with him?"

Nils eyed me. "The *Conyers* works harder'n any, but the pay is good an' she feeds well. Never mind the cap'n if you watch your tongue an' do your job. Only man to keep in mind is the bosun. He's a stomper."

My gills were dry as we plodded on along Front Street.

II

FOR THOSE who do not know much about seafaring before the wind, a bark, which is not short for barkentine, is considered a full square-rigger, having mostly square sails, with fewer, smaller fore-and-aft (schooner) sails. A barkentine, on the other hand, has a combination of square sails and equally large schooner sails. Even on the Banks, people sometimes mixed them up, saying "barkentine" when the ship lying off was actually a full-fledged square-rigger, as was the *Conyers*. A pure windjammer.

Soon I stood on the pitch-seamed, scrubbed

deck of Cap'n Reddy's vessel, seabag at my feet, and looked up the tall masts—fore, main, mizzen, and after, with crossing spars, the yards— mouth wide open, wondering if I'd have the hardiness to climb clear to the royals, the topsails of all. The rest of the crew had already disappeared forward with their gear.

In a moment of cherished dream, I could almost see myself up there on a yardarm, the captain shouting to me, "Ben, give a look to that lee mizzen brace."

"Aye, aye, sir." A fond hope, perhaps to come true.

"Vel, vat you doin' standin'?" yelled the bosun, looming suddenly. "Go to de Bravaman."

I had no idea what a Bravaman was, nor his location. I was struck speechless as the bucko mate glared down at me.

"Go to de fo'c'sle," Gebbert roared, lifting a boot toe, and I scurried that way. I well knew what the fo'c'sle was: the forecastle, or forward house, near the bow, where the crew lived.

En route, I chanced on the skinny sailor who'd given me the high sign not to dare come aboard the previous day, and learned his name was Barney. He came from a place called Jersey City.

"You did it, anyway," he said. "You'll be sorry."

"Had to," I replied, and quickly explained about Reuben down in the Caribbean.

"Watch out for that bosun," he warned.

I said I surely would.

In a moment, the two tipsy sailors came by, laughing and joking. That lasted just long enough for the bosun to grab them both by their collars and run down the deck with them full bore. Just before he reached the afterhouse, he let go of them. They drove on into the wood, their heads hitting like ripe melons, or so it sounded. They fell back on their behinds.

The bosun said to them, "Sober up."

Yes, he was a man to watch out for, I thought as I continued uneasily on to the fo'c'sle in search of the Bravaman, and I soon found him in the galley, which was mostly occupied by a big, six-hole coal range. A sink, chopping block, food shelves, and lockers took up the rest of it. On one bulkhead—wall—was a small statue of the Virgin Mary.

Meeting up with a Bravaman was to see some-one smoking a long cigar, short and tubby, dark of skin, hair, and eyes, wearing a stained towel around his neck beneath which hung a small gold cross on a chain. I stood there nervously and said I was the new boy. He looked me over and said something like "Bong dia." That was not the way we spoke on the Banks, and I had no answer.

He laughed and said, "You work for me, you learn Portuguese." And that's exactly what *bong dia* was, just a cheerful good morning. That ship was full of foreigners and I won't attempt to spell it out the way he talked. His *j*'s sounded like *s*'s; so did his *g*'s. His voice rose and fell like fast tides. "In" was "om" and "bom" was "bong."

Anyhow, Eddie Cartaxo had bad feet and limped along the deck as he took me aft. Every-one called him either Eddie or the Bravaman, the latter because he was from Brava, in the Cape Verde Islands, of which I'd never heard. They were off Dakar, Africa, he said, another far place.

Finally he showed me my bunk, and my mouth sagged.

———

Despite the maze of stout wire rigging, the spotless *Conyers* was a very simple but rugged ship, made of white oak and yellow pine, held together by galvanized-iron bolts. On the port side of the fo'c'sle was the galley; directly forward of it were two cabins filled with crew bunks and an eating table. On the starboard was the donkey steam engine and the carpenter shop. The donkey engine powered the windlass to raise the anchor, ran the pumps, and could hoist sails if Cap'n Reddy so chose.

Just ahead of the forward house, down a small hatch, was storage space for paint, tar, oil, rope, salt meat, coal, and other things. The anchor chain locker was up there, too. The cargo hatches, already battened down, were between the fo'c'sle and the afterhouse.

The fine tongue-and-groove afterhouse, just forward of the great, spoked helm (the steering wheel), was a little lower than the fo'c'sle. Entry was down a five-step companionway. In the paneled afterhouse was the captain's bedroom, with a double bed; bathroom, with a full-sized porcelain tub; chartroom; after cabin, in which rested the Chicago-made organ, bolted down; a dining saloon and rooms for the mates, bosun, and Eddie; a spare room for passengers. All in shining mahogany.

Then there was the narrow pantry, between the ice chest and the bosun's room, with a sink and serving board. Shelves with dishes and glasses, bowls and platters, tea and biscuit tins lined either side of it thwartships, and on the starboard side, beneath a square-window port, was a small bunk on which rode an old straw mattress and a dirty pillow. It was there I was to exist, among a thousand different smells, right under the bosun's nose. With mixed feelings, I unpacked and then went forward.

The galley range was firing up for dinner, and the Bravaman instructed, "Fill the coal bin but don't get any dust on deck. That bosun'll throw you in the chain locker and let the anchor loose." Him again.

So I began carefully lugging the soft Pocahontas nuggets up the ladder and out the forward hatch, holding the canvas bag tightly, keeping a weather eye open for Johann Gebbert. No longer was there any doubt about that German.

I will not bother with all the details of that long, confused day, but I spent a good part of it peeling potatoes while the *Conyers* was being prepared for sea. I well remembered that the official paper on Parley Bakerby's table said each crew member would receive one pound per day. By my calculation, I would skin upward of one hundred forty pounds a week, hardly my idea of sailors' work. Nor was feeding the captain's cat, cleaning his bathtub (about which he was finicky), making his bed, and dusting his cabin, as well as serving all meals aft. Those chores, among others, was what a steward's boy did, according to the Bravaman. Why didn't they just call it a trash-fish servant?

Sitting in the river breeze on the after side of the fo'c'sle, just outside the sliding galley door, peeling away, I thought of Tee and Boo to get my mind off *batatas,* as Eddie called them. Soon this day, the pair would be arriving in New York City, a place Tee had previously visited. She'd check into a fine hotel and then make arrangements for her passage. Already, she was living the life of ease, as was the hound. With each passing moment, I was more and more sorry that I hadn't put more stock in going to the N&W yards, as Mrs. Crowe had suggested. Or I wouldn't have minded a job polishing that Winton automobile.

About four o'clock, I finished approximately twenty pounds of Northern Neck spuds, and the rest of the sundown time was devoted to feeding the captain (he barely acknowledged me) and his spooky-eyed Siamese cat, plus the mates. Then I washed the supper dishes and cleaned the pantry and went forward again to help the Bravaman.

While doing so, I said to Eddie, "You sure are dark."

"My mother was Senegambian and my father white Portuguese, but there is also Moorish blood on my mother's side." I wasn't sure what a Senegambian or a Moor was, but we had some half Arabs on the Banks and maybe that was close. The Wahabs, shipwrecked in the 1700s, were on the brown side.

"I'm cockney British and Irish mixture, so I'm told," I said. "Not a person on those Banks that wasn't originally thrown ashore. All castaways."

Eddie laughed. "Everyone has to be something."

"These Verde Islands, where exactly are they?" I asked.

"About two hundred miles off Dakar, about sixteen hundred to Brazil. How they ever got named green I don't know. There are many volcanos. Fogo, not my home, is the Island of Fire, with a volcano ten thousand feet high, always smoking."

"Never seen a volcano," I said.

"Well, you come to Cape de Verdes, you'll see them. Many beaches have black sand instead of white sand. But in the valleys, out of the wind, where I live, it is green, and we grow yams and oranges and tobacco. In two more trips, I'll go back to my wife and children. We have a nice stone house—volcano rock—with a thatch roof."

"What'll you do then?"

"Farm and fish. Brava, the southmost island, is good for that."

I put down the Cape de Verdes as another place to go sometime on my journeys, especially that Fogo.

About eight-thirty, the bosun stuck his head into the galley. He asked Eddie whether or not the passenger cabin was clean.

Eddie replied, *"Está bem,"* which I took to mean yes, or something like that.

Gebbert said, "Vee got some people comin' aboard tonight."

Eddie said, "I hope they like stew."

I couldn't have cared less. Never so exhausted in my life, I got into my bunk in that stuffy pantry about nine o'clock and was asleep before I could think of anything more than aching muscles.

All the great sails had been bent on, ready for hoisting. All the cargo, food, water, and ice were aboard. Crew and officers and weary steward's boy aboard.

We'd voyage on the morrow.

12

Cap'n Reddy shouted, "Single up fore 'n' aft," meaning to take most of the lines off the dock, ready the ship for easing out into the channel.

Though I'd been on the move since 4 A.M., helping the Bravaman in the galley, any pesky doubts I'd had about the glories of the sea had vanished just after orange sunrise, when the tug *Mary Clark,* of the Joseph Clark Towing Company, came alongside. Feeling tingly all over, I now knew positively what Reuben had meant when he talked about it briefly. It was deep in the salt of my blood, this call of the wind and waves.

Yet I had no idea what to do. Already the bosun had almost run me down when taking the tug hawser aboard. All hands were turned out and busy.

The Bravaman was outside the galley, looking on, having coffee, and I inquired as to how I might best be of help. "Stay out of the way," he advised, which is not what I had in mind.

Then Cap'n Reddy shouted deep-voiced to a shabby handler ashore, "Let 'er go," and we were free of land at last, already slowly headed for the channel.

Try as I might, I cannot adequately describe how I felt that Friday morning as the *Conyers* put to sea behind the puffing *Mary Clark*. As I stood near the bow, I would have given anything to wave aloofly to Kilbie Oden and Frank Scarborough, two boys surely convicted to the land. It would also have been nice to see Tee standing on the dock, misty-eyed yet proud of me. Wool cap at a jaunty angle, I'd put on my seaboots for the occasion despite the fact that not a drop of water was falling anywhere. I did not care. Caught in the rapture of these thoughts, I was almost bowled over again when the bosun, howling with rage, came up to the bow to shift the towing hawser forward. The tug was moving out ahead of us as we rippled down the river.

"Ola," yelled the Bravaman, and crooked a finger my way. "Come into the galley so the bosun will not stomp you."

Right then, I died a little.

As the *Conyers* went regally downstream toward Hampton Roads, past Lambert's Point and Craney Island light, I was fretting and scrubbing pans. Just about opposite the nub of land on which was later to rest the world-famous Jamestown Exposition of 1907, the captain's yell of "Set upper tops'ls," which were about midway up the masts, echoed throughout the ship like a cry from Chris Columbus. Tears were near as I banged those pans around.

A few minutes later, Cap'n Reddy shouted again: "Sheet home the lower tops'ls; clap on the heads'ils."

I felt unmerciful agony.

A departure so stirring and thrilling that it deserved to be painted and framed forever, and I was awash in soapsuds. Then I heard the legendary chanteys begin and pleaded, "Eddie . . ."

He finally wiped his hands on the towel and nodded. "Now you can help," he said, limping out himself to boss some greenhorn sailors on the foresail.

There were men on the capstan—the round deck windlass—bending at the oak spars; others hauled on lines, and the chanteyman, old Frank, ship's carpenter, was singsonging "Away to Rio," each "yup" sending sail higher. Canvas was spreading; chief mate forward, second mate aft, captain by the helmsman, bosun moving all over the ship.

I glanced back at Josiah Reddy. He did not seem to be an earthly creature. In full uniform, gold stripes on his sleeves, he stood by the big double wheel, hands tucked in his double-breasted coat pockets, watching ahead and aloft. On the pug face was a special look: We were all about to ascend to Neptune's paradise. A moderate breeze was crooning down from the north, freshening, and I had, at long last, gone to mariner's heaven.

Setting topgallants and royals, I soon found myself hauling on lines with eight sailors, yelling "yup" just right with them as the chanteyman hit the "Up she rises."

Reuben, liking more to taste farm dirt in his mouth on his visits home, not talking too much about the sea, had never told me there were short-haul chanteys and long-haul chanteys, the pull changing from hefty, short drags to long, steady pulling, the chantyman changing his song and rhythm at the same time. "Haul on the Bowline" when sheeting home, "What to Do with a Drunken Sailor" and "Paddy Doyle" when the sail was stiff.

I can hear it now, out of the brilliant past. "Up she rises!" O, glory.

Soon the tug was cast off, and the magnificent *Christine Conyers,* under full sail, stood out to sea and took final departure on Cape Henry.

Never will I forget that glorious morning and never will I forget what happened that early afternoon as the crew was *sweating up* (tightening the halyards, you see) and making everything secure for sea. About two-thirty, with the *Conyers* scudding southeast at six knots, lifting on the swells; the ring of the chanteyman still in my ears, fresh perfume of salt in my nose, rigging singing, I came up out of the forward hatch with a bag of coal and happened to look aft.

I froze. Sand ghosties had risen by the after-house. I almost dropped the coal bag. *It wouldn't happen; it couldn't happen.* But it had, as predictable as the sunrise.

The British castaway girl saw me, then smiled widely and waved gaily. By her was a big, gold dog.

We were already fifteen miles out, fully rigged and bound for the Caribbean. The tugboat was long gone. So was my career.

I ran into the galley, dumped the coal bag, then streaked down the deck to confront her. My voice understandably cracked from pure emotion as I asked, "Why, Tee? Why did you do it?" Nothing like this had ever happened to me; I doubt to any other boy on his first professional voyage.

"Aren't you glad to see us?" she asked, mouth remaining open as if she'd never considered otherwise.

I said, "No! I'd rather see the devil. Why did you do it, Teetoncey?"

She then said, quite seriously, one of those things of which she was becoming very capable: "I couldn't stand to think of you going to Barbados alone on a hellship. You know nothing about Bridgetown."

All too true, but not much of a reason to follow me to sea.

I gathered myself together and made a wise decision. I said, "You two are nothing but common stowaways and I want nothing to do with you. I'll deny I ever saw you in my life."

I could see the change coming over her, like frost gathering on a moonless night. She replied, very coldly, "We aren't common stowaways. I paid the captain twelve dollars for my passage; four for Boo's. I thought you'd be glad to see us."

"I am not."

"You should be," she said, eyes smarting.

Now shaking with rage, I asked, "How did you talk the cap'n into it?"

"I told him I was going to visit my uncle Salisbury in Bridgetown."

What a rotten lie! She hated her uncle and he wasn't in Bridgetown.

"I'm a British subject, Ben. I have all my papers. I can visit any British possession in the world without your help." Calm and calculating as a swamp lynx she was, and just as sneaky. That girl had changed completely in ten days, or else she had hidden her true nature from us all.

I looked at the dog. How I ever came to love him and tend him as a puppy, I don't know. He had turned into the most unfaithful, troublesome ingrate on earth; cause of everything.

She spoke again. "I'm sorry you don't appreciate what we've done."

"Hah," I said, in no way sympathetic to her feelings at this point. Making effort not to yell, I got up close to her sharp nose and said, "I warn you, Tee, you don't know me. Neither does that dog. You're both on your own."

With that, I turned heels-about and headed back for the galley. She would be the complete ruin of me yet, and had made an awfully good start. I remember pausing outside the galley door and looking over toward the coast. Though easting, we were sailing along about opposite the Virginia border. During the night, we would pass Oregon Inlet, Bodie Island Lighthouse, and Heron Head Shoal, where this had all begun. It entered my mind to launch the yawl, which was chocked down aft, and return to the peace and comfort of the Hatteras shore.

Later in the day, when the sun was in its fourth quadrant to the west, I was sitting outside the galley peeling potatoes, feeling very low, when Tee strolled up with Boo. She had him on a length of rope.

"Good afternoon," she said as if shopping at the greengrocer's and definitely with some sort of female vengeance on her tricky mind. "You're the galley boy, aren't you?"

Oh, ho, she was going to play her evil game to

the hilt. I looked all about me, seeing no one near, and then asked, in a plainly hostile voice, "What are you doing up here?"

"I'm on my promenade, with my dog."

I glared at her. "What's a promenade?"

"A walk, a stroll about deck. Passengers do that often."

I could only think this was going to be a wearing voyage beyond compare. I said, "Tee, how could you tell the cap'n so many lies at one standing?"

Her smile was chalky. "Would you like me to tell him *one* truth?"

"No," I said, immediately realizing what she meant. That one could destroy me. No matter how much I protested, Cap'n Reddy would be sure to believe I'd been responsible for them coming aboard; certain to think I'd done it for romance or worse. "No," I repeated.

For more than an hour over the potato tub, I'd been trying to figure out when she'd come aboard; how she'd worked her conspiracy on the captain. I asked about that.

"I did it properly. I went to Hudgins & Hurst and waited for the captain. When he came in to pay for his supplies, I discussed the matter with him. It was all done in a few minutes."

"When did you come aboard?" I asked.

"Last night, of course. But I certainly didn't want to disturb you." She was always thoughtful.

"And you stayed in your cabin until we were well offshore?"

"Yes, we were both very tired, Ben. It had been a long day." That was true. She'd been up at five to sneak away from Mrs. Crowe's.

I shook my head in frustration. For the sake of everyone, that girl should have remained in her catatonic state, which was her frame of mind when Boo found her sprawled out on the November beach. It was only March, and I felt fifty years older.

"Did you tell the cap'n you were a fugitive from justice?" I asked, thinking that might bust her bubble.

"The subject didn't arise," Tee answered, not at all shaken.

I sat there looking at her for a while and then said, "One thing is certain, and it is this: You and I part company in the Barbadoes. Forever."

Tee replied tartly, "How can we part company if we've never been together?"

At every turn she was sticking her long pins into me, for no good reason, and I was just about to chase her away when the bosun came lunging up, screaming about coal dust on the deck outside the forward hatch. Grabbing me by the collar, jerking me up, letting loose a few German oaths first, he roared, "You swab de deck til dere iss not a speck in sight."

Gasping for breath, I nodded.

Just then, Tee addressed him, saying something like *"Sprechen Sie Deutsch?"*

I was slowly released to my feet as he turned toward her, very surprised. *"Ja,"* he said, and with new interest.

Then she began to rattle it out, and they talked for about ten minutes by my pile of potatoes. I just sat there and held my head. She'd won another heart.

The bosun finally said something like, *"Danke, Fräulein, auf baldiges Wiedersehen,"* and departed, smiling for the first time since I'd seen him. A smile on that porker face was the same as cracks in old concrete.

Feeling like a mudsucker's bottom fin, I asked, "What did he just say?"

"'Thank you, lady, see you later.'" Then she smiled sweetly down at me. "No one had spoken German to him for a long time. Such a nice man."

I had to know, and asked tiredly, "Tee, how did you learn to speak German?"

"From Muttie, our cook," she replied. "She's from Berlin and has been with us for ages. But I really don't speak German very well. My French is much better."

"Oh, I didn't know that," I said as cuttingly as I could.

"Heavens, it's teatime," she said, and did a little good-bye wave with her fingers, a toodle-oo, I suppose, and then continued on her promenade with that dog, nodding and smiling to everyone on deck.

13

ABOUT SUNDOWN, with the *Conyers* racing east
and south in fine weather, every sail bellied out,
the Bravaman began serving supper to the crew
through the "pie hole," which is a small, sliding-
door space in the bulkhead separating the galley
from the crew's quarters. He pounded on the
wood wall and yelled, "Come 'n' get it."

At the same time, I began making my trips to
the afterhouse with warmers of food, balancing
against the plunge and twist of the ship. To those
who have never sailed as a galley boy on a four-
master bark, you take the hot food aft, then dish

it out on plates and platters in the pantry, then serve it. Then keep your mouth shut. And who was sitting at the table in the dining saloon with the captain, mates, and bosun? Tee. Who else?

And over at one side of that splendid cabin slept Boo Dog, contentedly alongside the cat. Anyone on the Outer Banks from Chicky village north to Pea Island, south to Hatteras Inlet, can testify that Boo chased cats in and out of wrecks, up and down lighthouse steps, all his life. Now he was two inches from that saffron-eyed, mangy old Siamese, and snoring.

What's more, I soon found out that he was using the cat's sandbox, which I had to empty daily, to the lee of the after cabin. On the Banks, Boo "went" everywhere, even on gravestones and the steps of the Hatteras meeting hall, and now, in less than a half day, she had trained him in nature's calling. I swear that girl was a witch.

As I placed the captain's plate down, he gave me a swift, upbringing look, and said, "Ladies first."

So I went around and put the plate down in front of Tee. She smiled at me and said, "Thank you, waiter; such good food," though she hadn't taken a bite.

As I was heading back to the pantry to get the captain's plate, she called after me, "Waiter, could I please have a pinch of mustard for this mutton."

I nodded, went inside the pantry, and shook.

After my own supper, which I ate alone, perched on a box in that narrow closet of shelves, I helped the Bravaman clean the galley up and finally went back out on deck about eight-thirty. Except the on-duty watch—lookout on the bow, helmsman, and the bosun—all the rest of the crew had bunked down.

There was a white slice of water at the bow, the sails were humming, and looking up through their ghostly sheeting, as the masts waved back and forth across the sky, were millions of stars. Far off to port was a faint, thin cut of light. Looming, crossing, and dying. I guessed it might be Hatteras Light. Time did pass. I'd climbed the lighthouse steps many a day. I let my eyes drift along the horizon, knowing that the Banks were there, hidden except for the light wand. I couldn't help but think of everyone. I even mustered a kind of wry laugh. If they only knew. Not only was Ben O'Neal, son of John and Rachel, abeam, but also the castaway girl and a well-known former duck dog. The directions of life could never be reckoned.

Then, for a while, I watched the captain. I'd heard he took a brisk walk each night, weather permitting. He walked almost the length of the ship, near the rail, feet not far from the waterway. Back and forth, hands behind his back. Somehow, he timed himself so that he was always heading up as the ship rose on a swell. He never seemed to go downhill.

This was more like it, I thought, as the great vessel plowed peacefully along. Salt spray reached up and spattered me.

By nine I was very sleepy and decided to turn in. Avoiding Josiah Reddy, I went down the portside to the afterhouse and was just about to enter the hatch when the bosun moved forward from near the compass glow on the poop deck. He said, "Stand by to pump das organ."

Pump the organ? At this hour? I was dead tired.

He growled, "Get below to pump das organ. Das cap'n recitals til ten ven it is smooth like dis."

Tee's room opened off the after cabin, and soon she came out, as Cap'n Reddy warmed up. He seemed to play very well but I could not see him. Sitting on a stool behind the organ, I pumped the Story & Clark lever until almost ten, thinking what Filene Midgett would have to say about this sorry performance of a ship's master. Filene would not allow a harmonica to be played in his station, much less a church organ.

I recall that Cap'n Reddy taught Tee the words to "Shenandoah" and "Away to Rio." They sang duet for a while. They were getting along famously, and I do think a rich orphan has many advantages.

At one point, she tinkled a laugh. "I could sail forever."

Not with me, I thought.

14

REUBEN HAD ONCE said that no one except the captain got much sleep on a ship. That remark had not been of interest at the time, but now I was beginning to regret ignoring it. The lookout on the twelve-to-four watch, the graveyard watch, took a few minutes from pacing back and forth on the bow to awaken the Bravaman at 3:45 A.M. and then routed me out, after which he awakened the next watch, the four-to-eight. I went stumbling forward along the dark, slick deck half asleep, not even looking at the sea or sails, thinking that this was a hellship, indeed. Unless I was going to a duck blind, six-thirty was a sensible hour to be awakened on the Banks.

Stumbling around, I got kindling wood going in the galley range, then added coal, and finally the Bravaman put the coffeepot on. I felt better after having a cup of it and a couple of biscuits, fare the new watch shared. Nobody said very much.

I asked the Bravaman if this happened every single day in the week and he mumbled that it did, at sea; then went about fixing oatmeal and frying ham, while I cracked eggs, one per man, though the officers could have as many as they wanted. Somehow I made it through to dawn, when the crew turned-to to begin the day's work by first hosing down the deck. Smoke spun out of the donkey boiler stack, and the pump pounded away.

It was a fine, sparkling morning, after all. We were crossing the Gulf Stream in light airs and the sea had turned a deep blue. Gobs of orange-yellow seaweed drifted along. Here and there were pink and blue Portuguese men-of-war—jellyfish with tiny sails. Billowing white clouds were far to east, gray on the bottom. A lovely day.

Going aft with breakfast for officers' country, laden pans of oatmeal, eggs, and ham, I was actually feeling good now, no longer sleepy. The time was about 7 A.M. when I entered the dining saloon.

There sat Tee, looking fresh; red ribbon in her daisy hair. In a dress I hadn't seen. "Good morning, waiter," she said brightly. By my estimate, she'd gone to bed shortly after ten. Likely, she'd aroused no earlier than six-thirty. She'd had a full, comfortable night on a cotton mattress while my bones had rested on the *donkey's breakfast,* so-called because it is made of lumpy straw.

I said, "Good morning," but not cheerfully.

She said, "Lovely day, isn't it?"

I answered, "Depends how much sleep you got," and went on into the pantry.

When I returned with her plate, she said, "That looks very nice, waiter, but might I please have an extra piece of that ham for my dog."

My dog. That did it. I said forcefully, "Teeton-cey, I'm not going to put up with much more of this."

I had no way of knowing that Gebbert had entered the saloon and was standing behind me. "Vat did you call her?" he asked.

I stammered something.

The bosun glared at me. "Vatch your tongue, boy." Then he turned to the girl. "If dis galley-svamper iss insulting you, Fräulein, let me know."

Tee quickly said, "Oh, no, Herr Gebbert, it was all my fault. I'm afraid he doesn't like to be called waiter."

"Vell, dat's vat he is, isn't he?"

I practically ran for the pantry to serve the bosun his food and get him out of there. Then I stood by the door at their every beck and call while they ate and chatted in the bosun's native tongue, which sounded like a lot of gargles to me.

When the bosun left, Tee lectured. "Ben, you must be careful. You'll get us both in trouble."

I nodded numbly, determined to keep my mouth shut.

Soon the captain came in; then the chief mate, whose name was Everett. They all talked about the nice weather; then Tee departed to take her morning promenade, wishing me a cheery, "Good day," as she went up the companionway with Boo.

"Such a sweet and refined little girl, and so intelligent," said the cap'n, and Chief Mate Everett agreed, as most mates do.

I laughed grimly to myself.

The cap'n went on with his loose talk. "Her parents were lost in a shipwreck recently, and she's going down to live with her favorite uncle in Bridgetown."

The mate clucked his tongue and shook his head sympathetically while wolfing his eggs.

Standing silently by the pantry door and listening to all this, I was sorely tempted to walk right up and straighten out some things about the captain's most admired passenger. Josiah Reddy had been hoodwinked.

Soon he departed to inspect the ship with white gloves, and I went about clearing the table, washing the dishes, and taking the dirty pans back to the galley, talking to myself for the first time in my life.

Midships, Tee smiled sweetly as I passed, murmuring, "Cheerio." I clung to my temper.

Men were aloft, working in the sunlight and fresh air, polishing brass on the yards. A few were painting here and there. One was repairing ratlines and battens. The chanteyman was doing his carpenter work, fixing a hatch coaming that had been damaged in loading cargo. The sailmaker sat in the golden light stitching on an inner jib split. And there was I, toting dirty pans, a lowlife galley-swamper, as Gebbert had said.

As I reached the foredeck, a sailor new to the *Conyers,* a big man, Perkins by name, complained about having to polish brass at sea with brick dust and oil. It was his ill luck to have Cap'n Reddy overhear. No sooner had Perkins voiced his dislike than the cap'n kicked out a locust-wood belaying pin with his heel, caught it in midair, and chased the big sailor up the mast, shouting for the bosun not to let him down till sunset.

Hellship for sure, I thought.

As I entered the galley, Eddie grinned. *"Que tal?"* He was usually in a good mood.

"What does that mean?" I asked, ready to chew a marlinspike myself.

"How goes it?"

"Bad," I said. "I can't wait to get off this ship in the Barbadoes."

"There's not much ashore there," he answered.

"Makes no difference to me. I'm prepared to sit in that port for a year and wait for my brother."

The Bravaman was slicing onions for a stew. "Well, you can't do that. We'll only be there two days and then sail for Rio."

"I'm only going as far as the Barbadoes," I informed Eddie. "And the next ship, I'm working with the crew. That's for sure. Not in any pantry." Another month of this and I'd be a tattered sponge. I wouldn't at all mind polishing brass out in the fresh air. My intentions now were to sign on with Reuben as quickly as possible.

The Bravaman rested his cleaver. "You're going to jump ship in Bridgetown? That is trouble."

"No, that's as far as I go."

Eddie shook his head. "Every man on here signed for the full voyage. You, too."

I just stood there, blinking. Now that I remembered, Parley Bakerby had signed me on with all the rest—Barbadoes, Rio de Janeiro, and pay off north of Hatteras. Nothing was going right.

Finishing the pans in a daze, I went aft again to square away the pantry, make the cap'n's bed, and scrub the ring from his bathtub; then scrub the decks in the dining saloon and after cabin with limewater. In the midst of the latter job, it suddenly occurred to me that, by staying on the *Conyers,* I could shed all responsibility for Tee and the dog. It would be fare thee well in Bridgetown. I could endure the drudgery to Rio and back.

The day brightened considerably.

In fact, when I next saw her, just before noon, I said, smiling widely, "And how are you today, Mistress Appleton?"

She frowned, sensing a change of attitude.

———

It took quite a while to cross the Gulf Stream under thin airs, all that day and into the night. Our course to the Windward Islands was an easy arc eastward and south, passing just west of Bermuda, easting as far as possible before getting down to the region of the northeast trades, so I heard Cap'n Reddy explain to Tee at supper. He would try to keep the wind behind him to take advantage of east winds as the *Conyers* got farther south. "I don't like to beat up against the winds," he said.

So attentive, she nodded her head as if she understood every bit of it. Even asked questions, such as "What winds prevail north of Bermuda?" as if it made any difference. She even asked, "Is that why they call it a dead nailer?" A southward wind, any fool would know. The cap'n was eating it up, along with his stew.

Another trying meal. Wouldn't you know he'd be carrying on a deep nautical conversation with that skinny, blond doily maker instead of me. Likely, it wouldn't have been so bad were it not that Tee managed to be on hand each time I made a mistake. If I skidded on deck and dumped a platter of pork chops, she was there.

"Could I be of assistance, waiter?"

"No."

If I forgot and spit to windward, she'd be not five feet away when the glob came flying back into my eye.

"Strong wind, isn't it?"

The mockery and japery continued on for four solid days.

15

ON THE FIFTH DAY, dawn came in with heavy black clouds to east; the sea had turned gray. The barometer reading sank, telling us that a gale of wind would soon hit. There was storm chill in the air, and it mounted slowly as the breeze picked up, making a fluttering arrow out of the wind pennant on the foremast.

Cap'n Reddy skipped organ recital that night to stand in rubber coat and sou'wester by the helmsman. Lightning was cracking out of every cloud, and the crew was turned out to furl the royals, the crossjack, and the flying jib. The *Con-yers* was beginning to pitch and roll.

A little later, Cap'n Reddy shouted, "All hands on deck. Stand by the t'gallant halyards." The order was echoed throughout the ship, and there was a thud of feet.

A moment later, the bosun shouted, "Lay aloft an' furl."

As spray drenched the fo'c'sle, I helped Eddie secure everything in the galley and then went aft, skidding back and forth across the deck, to wedge the plates and platters in the pantry, tie down the tins.

Coming back into the saloon a few minutes after nine, I found Tee sitting there, face pinched and white, hands clenched on the dining table. She was disarranged. There wasn't much doubt why. It hadn't been six months since the *Malta Empress* wrecked. She couldn't help but be remembering how it was in the *Empress* saloon when that ship rolled and pitched and creaked and screamed, finally to stagger on Heron Head Shoal and come apart.

Uneasy myself, I went up to her and sat down. "Don't be frightened, Tee," I said.

She nodded, but each time the ship rode up and then pounded down drunkenly, she winced. Her lips were pearl-colored, and she kept swallowing.

I said, "This is a bigger and better ship than the *Empress* ever was."

Then the tears began to leak down, and she suddenly tore away from the table, running into her cabin. I went after her but heard the door lock. I said, "Tee, let me come in and stay with you."

She wouldn't answer.

Finally, I put on my oilskins and boots, then went out to stand in the lee of the afterhouse cabin trunk, the little house over the after companionway, not too far from the helm, which now required two sailors. It kicked every time the *Conyers*'s stern rose out of the water. Cap'n Reddy stood with his back to the taffrail, riding the bucking stern. Only when blue-white streaks lit the ship up could I see his face. Rain was hitting like bullets, but he seemed relaxed, and I felt better.

Now and then there were yells from the rigging, and as the lightning stabbed out, I could see Gebbert and his men up there, hanging on as they furled sail. With each roll of the ship, the masts walked across the boiling sky. It was a night of "one hand for the ship and one hand for yourself."

Though I hate to admit it, watching, I suddenly realized that it was too soon for me to join them up there. A slip of foot and they'd plunge more than a hundred feet to deck or into the sea. Until this very moment, I'd never doubted my ability. I did now. It was a sobering sight. I wouldn't have gone aloft that night for two Wintons, and a Haynes-Apperson thrown in.

I stayed out there a while longer, then went below, being of absolutely no use. Knocking on Tee's door, I asked, "All right in there?"

A weak "Yes" came back, and I asked if I could come on in. She said, "I'd rather not."

So I went to the pantry, undressed, and got into the bunk, listening to the wild night outside, feeling the hull quiver and shudder as it entered the gale; heard the wash and then booms of the sea. Every joint in the *Conyers* was creaking and grinding.

Hanging on for dear life, I fell asleep about midnight.

Awakened just before four, I went topside in time to see the crew furling the mainsail. Lifelines had been rigged along the deck, as water was washing ankle- to knee-deep from stem to stern, the *Conyers* scooping it up as she dug into waves. She was burying the angel figurehead in froth, harpooning the mountainous seas with her jibboom.

Feeling queasy, I started to fire up the range. The Bravaman, hanging on with one hand, working with the other, said, "Don't bother. We can't cook." He told me to slice up some cold salt pork to serve with bread. I soon nicked my finger, and a moment later was hanging on to the fo'c'sle after railing feeding the fish, so to speak. My innards almost came up.

This time, Tee was not in sight.

With dense streaks of foam on the sea, edges of wave crests breaking into spindrift, the gale pounded the *Conyers* all of that day and night.

No hot food was served, only salt pork and salt beef and biscuits. We sailed quite a distance under bare masts; then the storm blew over, leaving an afterswell that rolled us back and forth. Being ill, and joined by many others, I didn't see much of Tee during this time. Only once did we talk. Her face was deathly pale and she broke down, saying she was so sorry for what she'd done—coming on board foolishly. I said to forget it; she hadn't done anything so bad, after all. We had looked our Maker in the eye and everyone was feeling respectful.

I now think that a good storm is good for a person, even for a ship. The dust of the mind is blown away and the air is cleared. The ship is tested, as are the men. The pure and simple rising of the sun is appreciated.

The next morning, the weather turned fair and warm, the sea oily and smooth. The planes of canvas, up again over the *Conyers,* flapped listlessly. We were becalmed, but it was not unwelcome. The crew tarred the rigging, patched sail, and made minor repairs as the big hot ball quickly dried us off. It was as if the Mother Sea had said of her storm, "I just wanted to remind you . . ."

At breakfast Tee smiled weakly at me. "Thank you, Ben, for everything."

"It wasn't anything," I said, and it hadn't been, just a few words of comfort now and then in her hour of need. The war between us was over, at least temporarily.

That whole day after we'd emerged from the storm and afterswell was a strange one—of looking back and ahead, of revelation. Somehow it seemed that the Mother Sea was in one of those resting moods on a quiet, pretty day, just letting us float along, saying to us, "Now I'll give you all some time to sort yourselves out . . ."

Midmorning, the bosun gave me billy hell for dropping some grease on the deck when I emptied the garbage at the stern, and I came back to the galley yelling about what a loudmouthed trash fish he was.

Eddie heard it all patiently and then he said, "Everybody hates him until . . ."

"Until what?" I asked.

"Until there is trouble." His dark eyes held me.

I scoffed at the tubby Portuguese and he shrugged. "Get Barney to tell you what happened two nights ago when you were asleep."

So I looked Barney up, and he said he'd slipped in the rigging ninety feet up and was hanging by one hand, and it was that monster Hans Gebbert who came out and got him, saved his life.

As I said, a good storm is good for a person, sometimes even for a ship.

Tee helped me peel potatoes in the early afternoon, and about three we crawled out on the jibboom, under the flapping heads'ils, over the bowsprit and the angel figurehead. There is no nicer place on any ship than over the bow, on that boom far out over the water. Under way, you can look down and see the prow, a white bone in its teeth, slicing the sea. Porpoise make runs on it.

Becalmed out there is nice, too. For some reason, when the sea is flat as paint, everyone lowers his voice. The ship becomes very quiet. There is only a slight slap of rigging, a barely heard creak as the timbers and hackmatack knee braces wear lazily.

I rigged a fishing line and hook, covering it

with white cloth, jigging it up and down, and soon had an amberjack on it. Aside from galley work, I full well realized now that I wasn't of too much use on that ship. But I did know how to fish.

After a while, I got to talking to Tee about us. I'd done some hard thinking in that bunk during the gale, before and after my prayers to save our souls, and I said, "We've got to tell the cap'n, you know. I mean, about you and me and our connection."

"I know," she said. "It was such a stupid thing for me to do."

Be that as it may, I said, "I bit off more than I could chew, too. I thought I was just coming to the Barbadoes to find Reuben. Now Eddie tells me I've got to go on to Rio. I signed on like everybody else."

"Then you must go," Tee said.

"What'll happen to you?"

"I'll get back to Norfolk." She laughed, a little nervously. "Then I'll go on to where I was supposed to go. Home."

My thoughts were troubled. I surely wanted to find Reuben, but I also felt I had a responsibility toward Tee, whether I wanted it or not. "I don't know what to do," I said.

Tee replied sensibly, "Well, why don't we start by telling the captain. Everything."

I didn't look forward to that, after seeing him chase that sailor up the mast. "He's not going to believe me. He'll be certain I asked you to come on here."

"It was all my fault. He'll believe me," she said.

I wasn't so sure. "Let's don't do it until a day out of Bridgetown." *An hour would be better,* I thought.

"Then we must."

I agreed, for better or worse.

About four o'clock, while I was jigging the fishing line, something hit like one of Mr. Stone's hotshot freights. The line began running out so fast that it burnt my palm until I got it down on the boom and stopped it off against the wood.

I yelled for help, and Nils, who was working up near the bow, climbed out, and about four-fifteen we horsed that thing in, carrying the line on back about midships. In not too long a time we looked down in the smooth, emerald water and saw an eight-foot shark. He'd swallowed the hook and had little chance to escape.

A cry of "Shark, shark," went up all over the *Conyers*. It was an omen. The captain's sprinkling of sugar on the water in the morning hadn't broken the calm, nor had his chantey. We now had a second chance.

With four of the crew helping, we got the shark up over the side and Nils dispatched him with a handspike, Boo losing his mind at the sight of the flopping fish. He barked himself hoarse, as he was inclined to do on the Hatteras beach when we hauled gill nets at sunset.

Cap'n Reddy came out of his quarters grinning. "We'll get a breeze now," he said confidently.

A tarpaulin was laid out on deck, and the Bravaman took his steaks off that big, white body, extracted the liver to fry it down for oil; then the rest of the man-eater went over the side.

Sure enough, about five-thirty the wind began to whisper; the flapping sails took hold, and the *Conyers*, after drifting most of the day, began to move again. So my stock was higher that night than it had been. The captain said five words to me, more than his usual one or two. There was shark steak, which tastes a little like swordfish, on the table.

For the fine days that followed, the wind stayed mostly to eastward, and Cap'n Reddy kept the square-rigger "full 'n' by," taking advantage of every breath of air. The horse latitudes, which we had entered, smiled upon us, and we had very few hours of calm. In the "horses," the 30-degree latitudes, the winds are often light and variable.

Tee talked a lot about what we would do when we got to the island. She wanted to show me the castle of the land pirate Sam Lord and the cannon on the beach at Speightstown; the breadfruit trees, courtesy of Captain Bligh and HMS *Bounty;* Cotton Tower, where the West Indies Regiment had a signal station; the Animal Flower Cave, Cole's Cave, Dawlish Cave; and the Redlegs, last of the Scottish slaves. I couldn't wait to make arrival.

I think everyone in the dining saloon and about deck noticed that Tee and I were friendly now.

16

On a sparkling, blue-skied morning two days out of the Barbadoes island, our sixteenth day at sea, all secrecy went splashing down, as was sure to happen, I suppose.

The island, just east of the Windwards, about opposite St. Vincent, below such islands as Martinique and Dominica and St. Lucia, above the Grenadines and Trinidad, places I fully intended to visit someday, was being reached on a gentle curve from the east, the *Conyers* making about four or five knots, sometimes six or more.

Preparing to enter port shipshape and spanking clean, the crew was holystoning the deck, adding spit and polish here and there. Busy, too; I remember that I was in the galley helping the Bravaman, and everything was going fine when Barney stuck his head in. "Brig comin' up on the starboard bow."

Just chatting, I had talked again to Barney about the *Elnora Langhans,* telling him all about Reuben and how much I hoped he'd be working cargo in Bridgetown when we arrived. So Barney was alerted to keep his owl eyes open for any brig that passed close aboard.

In high excitement and anticipation, I ran down the hot deck to the helm. The captain's long glass was in a locker space near the binnacle, the compass box, and I yanked it out without even asking permission.

The helmsman yelled, "Hey, bring that back." Nobody but the captain and the mates were supposed to touch that long glass.

I paid him no mind, raced to the bow, and focused on the brig, which was under all plain sail.

I raked along the vessel with the glass and finally had the circle on the bow nameplate, which was just forward of the snugged-home anchor.

To be sure, it was the *Elnora Langhans,* two-masted and square-sailed, with schooner sails aft; heads'ils all spread and bellied; white bone in her teeth, as pretty a brig as I'd ever viewed. The Mother Sea had worked in her mysterious way, fating that Reuben's course would pass close to mine.

Naturally, I went flying back toward the stern, yelling, "Stop the ship! Stop the ship!"

Such confusion as you've never seen hit the *Christine Conyers.* From aloft and up and down the deck, sailors began shouting, "Man overboard," which wasn't the case at all. The bosun grabbed a line and dashed toward the stern to heave it out to the unlucky sailor. Two or three seamen climbed up to ready the yawl for launching.

Tee came out of the afterhouse, and I yelled at her, jumping up and down. "Reuben's out there. That's the *Langhans.*"

Cap'n Reddy quickly appeared, too. "What 'n hell is goin' on?" he bellowed.

I barely made sense. "Stop the ship, Cap'n. My brother's on that brig."

"What are you doing with my long glass?" was his second bellow.

I didn't bother to answer that, just whooped again, "Reuben's on there," as he ripped the long glass from me.

Fuming, the captain cupped his hands around his mouth to shout, "Belay man overboard! Belay man overboard." Cancel the alarm, that meant; and I heard some choice curses fore to aft.

Despite his rage, the cap'n still said to the helmsman, "Bring her up a bit. Easy, now."

It is an old tradition of the sea, thank goodness, especially under sail, to greet another vessel; ask her destination and compare positions from the last sextant sight. If a friend of crew or captain is aboard the passing vessel, other welcome words are exchanged.

Cap'n Reddy would not deny the ancient tradition, but I made the mistake of asking "Are you going to stop the ship?"

He almost blew me down. "No, you idiot. We'll pass her close in."

I had to be grateful for that.

So I ran back to the bow to take advantage of every second as we glided past the *Elnora Langhans*. We were now closing rapidly as the captain pulled the *Conyers* eastward, and it looked as though there wouldn't be more than three or four hundred feet between us. The *Langhans* altered course, too, to come within hailing distance. All of her crew was up on deck, as was ours. What a thrilling event!

Finally, I saw Reuben, and my heart pounded. For a few seconds, I thought I might cry. There he was, by the forward rail, lean and trim, with Mama's big nose, looking not much different from how I'd seen him the spring before. A true Heron Head man.

When our bows were just about opposite, the *Langhans* bent north, the *Conyers* headed south, I yelled, "Reuben O'Neal! It's me, your brother Ben."

There was a moment of stunned silence. Then Reuben shouted back, "Ben, what are you doing in that ship?"

"I'm going to the Barbadoes."

"You lost your mind?" he yelled.

By now, the ships were passing swiftly and there'd be precious little time to talk to him. I began moving down the deck toward the stern. He was moving toward his stern, too, keeping pace.

"Nope," I shouted proudly. "I'm a seaman now. How are you?"

"Fine. How's Mama?"

I just couldn't do it. I couldn't tell him she was dead and gone in those few seconds. Wherever I got presence of mind, I don't know, but I yelled, "Mama'll be glad to know I saw you." And she would have been.

"You should be back home, Ben," he hollered.

"Where are you bound?" I asked.

"Port Fernandino. Ben, you get your tail back home where you belong and off these ships." That was big brother Reuben, all right, looking out for my welfare.

Then the first of two ordained disasters struck. Boo Dog, who must have been having his usual morning sleep somewhere on that warm deck, had awakened. Not only from the excitement of the ship passing but likely because he recognized Reuben O'Neal, he began yelping and running along, too, by my legs.

Reuben shouted over. "Is that Boo Dog?"

Not thinking, not a dollop of thought about identifying myself with that dooming hound, I yelled back happily, "Sure is."

Reuben, completely mystified by now, shouted, "Ben, you better write an' tell me what this is all about."

By this time, we were almost cleared and I was going at full gallop, headed for the after rail to say my last words. No more than a yard from it, Boo got under my feet and I went over the stern sideways, like a grape popped from a hull.

It was indeed quite a jolt to find myself spread-eagled in the air and then plunging down into the warm Atlantic Ocean.

I bobbed up again, and the last I saw of the *Elnora Langhans,* Reuben was on the stern, laughing his head off and waving good-bye. From where he stood, I guess it was very funny. From where I was, fun was not it. The *Conyers* was drawing away, Boo barking at me from the taffrail as if I'd jumped in for pleasure.

For several reasons, I am sorry to say that Cap'n Reddy did have to stop his ship, after all. Treading water, I heard that foghorn voice thunder out, "Fool overboard. All main yards aback."

He was a very fine seaman.

17

ABOUT AN HOUR later, dried off now, I stood worriedly outside the captain's stateroom with Tee and the worst Jonah who ever put to sea. We'd been squirming around three or four minutes, but there was no use in putting it off. I knocked very lightly, hoping the *Conyers* master was taking a morning nap. No such luck. There was an answering, and we went in.

At his desk, turning in his chair, he looked at the three of us for a long time, gray eyes appearing to come out of lightly smoking brick kilns.

He was in a dangerous state that we Outer Bankers call a "cold bile." At last, he spoke and directly to me. "Falling overboard is either an act of God or of stupidity, and I can't charge you for the former. You cost me an hour of running time."

Without hesitation, I said, "I'll pay for it, Cap'n."

His brief laugh was like a rusty nail, square at that, being pulled out of oak heart.

Boo suddenly twisted around and began to bite at fleas in the section where his tail joined his body. His teeth clacked and he made a wet, slobbering noise, calling attention to himself at the worst possible time.

The captain studied him a moment and then said, "During all that nonsense on deck, I heard your brother make reference to that dog. Now, how would he know him? I understood the dog belongs to this young lady. I made the mistake of not inquiring his history."

Some history, Boo had. Nonetheless, trapped all the way, I began, "Well, Cap'n—"

Josiah Reddy interrupted me sharply to let us know his current frame of mind. "Someone on this ship has been lying and I don't take kindly to that."

Mindable of exactly what he meant, I looked over at Tee and she nodded. It was past time to tell the painful truth in that spit-and-polish cabin before a royal king of the ocean. So I began the night when the *Malta Empress* hit Heron shore, washing Teetoncey up half frozen, and she took it from where Consul Calderham met her at the EC&N train arrival in Norfolk almost a month ago. We left nothing, or very little, out.

Meanwhile, the chief culprit sprawled down comfortably and slept through most of it, awakening now and then to dig under his chin with a hind paw. Fleas gathered there and back on his flanks, mostly.

The master of the *Conyers* did not sleep. His nutmeg face went from interest and sympathy when I talked about the *Empress* wreck and Tee's speechless condition to disbelief when I discussed attempting to salvage the hundred thousand dollars in silver off Heron bar; back to true sympathy when I told him about Mama. Tee's story of how she maneuvered in getting aboard did not make him happy. He had been fooled by her and didn't exactly appreciate it, orphan or not. To finish, I made a short defense in our behalf by saying we came from good folks: Tee's mama and mine were fine, upstanding women; Tee's papa had been a plantation owner in the Barbadoes and a barrister in England; mine was a heroic surfman. It was just that we had all been the victims of circumstance and a bumbling dog.

At the end of this long hour, Cap'n Reddy seemed limp. He said wearily, "Just go. I have to think about this. I've been sailing forty-six years and thought I'd heard everything."

Outside the door, Tee sighed deeply. "I feel better now, Ben."

I did, too. For a while.

I quickly learned that when a sailor makes a fool of himself ashore, falls off a barstool, or gets knocked into the sawdust, everyone laughs and talks about it for days, but when a sailor makes a fool of himself at sea, such as stumbling overboard, silence follows as if everyone is embarrassed, including the vessel. I was barely spoken to at dinner, and the same existed at supper. Tee didn't fare much better. Even the bosun was cool to her. By and large, we were ignored and outcasted. The story had gotten around. We had conspired to hoodwink Cap'n Reddy, and I had caused the crew extra work in stopping the ship. I also think there were some suspicions about me bringing Tee aboard for ulterior reasons.

Immediately after supper, Tee went to her cabin and I cleaned the pantry, then went forward to complete my chores in the galley, where the Bravaman didn't have much to say, either.

I kept to myself that entire evening and finally sat up on top of the fo'c'sle house until late, looking at the stars and wishing I'd never heard of the prettiest four-master bark from Cape Race to the Horn.

The captain was taking his nightly stroll, pacing as usual with his hands behind his back, and after a while he walked up to me. I jumped down, legs trembling a little. Not again, I hoped.

"You said your papa was a surfboat captain."

"Yessir. Lifesaver. He went out to vessels in distress, no matter the waves. That's what killed him. Big surf."

"Where did he serve?"

"Hatteras Banks, sir."

"How did he die?"

"His boat capsized. A ship had broken up in a gale of wind."

I could barely see Cap'n Reddy's face, so I didn't know what expression was on it, and I wasn't prepared for what he had to say next.

"If I can get a man to replace you, you can pay off in Bridgetown. I think you should try to get that little girl safely back to Norfolk."

I said, "Yessir, but I'm ready to go on to Rio, and pay my debt."

He was silent.

I said, "I'm sorry about today, Cap'n. I won't make that mistake again."

"Not likely," he answered.

I said, "I want to work off that hour of running time that I cost."

He replied, "I've canceled that debt. More things than one have been lost at sea. When you get back to the Banks, which I hope will be soon, tell the surfmen the master of the *Conyers* sends his respects and regards." Then he walked away.

I stood there a long time, wondering exactly what he meant when he said, "More things than one have been lost at sea." I've come to believe he was talking about all the John O'Neals. They'd canceled many a debt in fifteen-foot surf.

In fact, just about four-thirty the next morning, when the coffee was beginning to bubble, I talked to the Bravaman about the captain's change of attitude toward me. Eddie said that all sailors had a warm spot in their hearts for surfmen. He further said that sailors who had to pass the Hatteras Banks in the dead of winter were especially sympathetic just because they were scared witless.

Therefore, my position was more favorable now that it was known who I was.

18

REUBEN LONG AGO said he was about to blow up and burst on his first sight of foreign soil, Cuba in '88, and it was the same with me that warm April morning when the Barbadoes island loomed over our port bow, with a few green mountains reaching up to touch drifting cotton clouds. Tee had me awaken her early, and now we stood in the fresh, moist, pink tropic light as the *Conyers,* full-sailed and heeling slightly, swept on toward the Atlantic coast of this easternmost of the fair Caribbees. On the lee side, out of the

Atlantic Ocean rollers and wind, was the lapping Caribbean Sea and the ports of Bridgetown and Speightstown.

Any good geography published around 1900 will tell you that the island, twenty-one miles long and fourteen wide, shaped like a shoe with toe to the north, is a slice of "rolling old England" and that one of Eddie Cartaxo's Portuguese ancestors first landed on it, when only the Arawak Indians were there, living in thick forests. The Carib Indians killed off all the Arawaks and then abandoned the island, because it didn't have too much freshwater. The British took it over about the time that a man from Brazil brought up a single sugarcane plant. Then the British hauled in black slaves and white slaves to clear the forests and work the plantations. Now and then the French and the Dutch tried to grab it.

Coconut trees ring the beaches, and there are such things as purple moonflower plants and jasmine and mamey apple and lime and pawpaw and sweetsop, along with a few monkeys. There are over five hundred stone-house windmills, nothing like our stilt-house corn mills on the Banks, and such things as yellow-breasted mustache birds and poisonous manchineel trees. The island got its name of *Los Barbados* (which means hairy) from the Portuguese because of the bearded fig trees that grow on inland cliffs. But I knew none of these things when I stood agog on the wet deck as Cap'n Reddy piloted the bark down on Bridgetown, tacking back and forth.

I had one advantage, though: the castaway girl. Pointing far off, she said, "That's Mount Hillaby, and all the valleys around it are filled with breadfruit and banana trees. And we can't see it yet, but Point Kitridge is over there." Last time she'd been to this place, her parents were alive, and I think she was having a mixture of memories, happy and sad, face holding a hint of shadow. Her finger went northwest. "And way around there is Bathsheba. This time every day, the Bajan flying-fish fleet goes to sea from Bathsheba, through the coral reefs." The finger went southwest. "And down that way, in Christ Church Parish, was our plantation . . ."

She faltered and I said quickly, "Tell me about the flying-fish fleet."

There wasn't much to tell: Each dawn, the boats went out to shoals far offshore, hung bags of spoiled, mashed crabs and bottom sprats into the water to make drifting oil, which attracted the flying fish into nets. It was said they were delicious broiled and topped with creole sauce or baked in fish pie. That island was world famous for its meals of flying fish.

Tee got over her memory tugs, but unfortunately I did not have long to stand out there and jabber and sightsee. After serving up breakfast, my usual drudge chores were demanded, no matter that the land grew larger every hour. Imagine being bent over the captain's bathtub, scrub rag in hand, when Sam Lord's castle appeared on shore about ten o'clock. Oh, I stole looks topside now and then, but there is no more grievous sentence, as any sailor can testify, than to be at work belowdecks when the four corners of the earth are unfolding not a crow's flight from the mainmast.

———

Running on in, we passed Foul Bay and Long Bay, and then rounded South Point on our steady way to old Bridgetown, founded somewhere around 1630; picked up Needham Point Lighthouse, a stubby beacon, and then went smartly into Carlisle Bay, outside the harbor and Careenage, dropping anchor and sails in early afternoon, a joyous moment. Officially, our voyage was logged in as completed at 1340 hours, April 4, 1899.

No sooner had the *Conyers* settled down on her chain than the Barbadian boatmen, six or eight of them, rowed up around the stern in their skiffs, shouting to the captain.

"Hey, Cap'n, you hire me, eh?"

"Oh, his boat will sink," said another. "You will drown. You must hire me."

"I 'ave the finest boat in this bay, an' I do thank you for just hiring me," yelled another.

Cap'n Reddy laughingly shouted back to them, "You're all a pack of rascals." He'd been to Bridgetown many times.

One boatman then yelled, "But, Cap'n, we are noble rascals."

"Aye," said Reddy, and there was more laughter. The boatmen would be used to go back and forth ashore, and visit other ships if necessary.

Bridgetown: I had made it safely. Had my sea legs. Salt was in my brow and I felt fine. The air was hot and smelled of sweet flowers. Despite some minor troubles, it had all worked out. We were together. Tee was beside me, with big Boo stationed at her feet, likely wondering what this was all about. I do doubt that any Banks hound had ever ventured so far, even by accident. To be sure, he would be the first dog from Heron Shoal ever to set paw on this particular slice of the British Empire, upon which the sun never sets. He gazed around, sniffing. The smells were new to him, too.

And had my own light and airy head been on a swivel, it would have rotated three hundred and sixty degrees. Over there, around a jetty, were the buildings of Bridgetown, and the busy inner port, with schooner masts sticking up. In the blue bay itself, fringed with wind-bent coconut palms, were eight or ten large ships, both sail and coal-burning, and I was quite surprised to see the Britisher *Cashamara,* a white-hulled steamer, swinging at hook not far from us. She'd left Norfolk a full three days after the *Conyers* and was already here, taking on bagged sugar brought out in small barges sculled by a long sweep. Not knowing where to look next, I had only one thing in mind: stepping foot on that warm Barbadoes earth. The Bravaman said that would be possible once we got health clearance.

So we waited.

19

In time, a boat rowed our way containing three officials of Her Majesty's government. I had never seen sailors such as the two bending at oars in the boat plainly marked HARBOUR POLICE. Flat straw hats were perched on their heads; queer uniforms from there down.

Tee knew, of course. "They're wearing the Jack Tars of Lord Nelson. Middie blouses and bell-bottoms. But they don't wear pigtails anymore."

"I'd hope not," I said, thinking that no man on the Banks would be caught dead in pigtails.

As we all watched, the three officials clambered up the accommodation ladder, wearing other clothes I'd never seen on any person. White short pants and white stockings. White helmets.

"Tropic dress, with pith helmets," said Tee. "Introduced from India regiments." There is nothing so educational as going to sea.

So far, it was a most unusual place, I thought, as the officials were greeted by Cap'n Reddy and disappeared into the afterhouse to do their business. Everyone on the *Conyers* was in good health, so the quarantine doctor had no problem clearing us and got back into the boat, which was replaced immediately with another police boat.

A few minutes later, I was looking forward to a skiff ride to the Queen's Dock when the bosun came trodding up to say, "You two, follow me. *Das Hund* stays here."

We did so, having no idea what was in store, down through the forward cabin behind Gebbert's lurching back, and directly into the captain's stateroom, where stood the two officials, cool as ice cream in their tropics; and Josiah Reddy, the latter frowning at us. About this time,

I had a sinking feeling. Tee's quick glance toward me was nervous. The bosun departed and the door was closed.

"Good afternoon," said the shortest of the two, knobby-kneed and rawboned and small-eyed. "I am Basil Collymore, Solicitor-General, Queen's Counsel, and this is Sergeant Marion Watkins, of Her Majesty's police. You are Miss Wendy Appleton, eh?" He peered at Tee with not much friendliness. Basil Collymore was white, and Sergeant Watkins was black.

I'd never heard Tee's voice so thin as when she answered, "Yes."

His eyes shifted, perch spotting the worm. "And you are Benjamin O'Neal, U.S. citizen, member of this ship's crew."

I nodded.

"I have here papers ordering that Miss Appleton be returned to the port of Norfolk, at the request of the British consul general, aboard any vessel bearing the Empire flag."

Breath out of us, we just stood there.

Basil Collymore went on, "And there's not to be any interference from you, young man."

Feeling puny and swallowing, I looked over and saw Tee's chin quivering. Her eyes had begun to well and her face was as white as Collymore's spotless shirt.

He passed the letter to her, saying, "You should read this, Miss Appleton, so you will clearly understand the seriousness of what you've done."

With shaking hands, she took it, and I looked over her shoulder:

Honourable Basil Collymore, Q.C., O.B.E., M.A.
Government House
Bridgetown,
Barbados
B.W.I.

In a low voice I asked Tee, "What is a solicitor-general?"

"Just below the attorney-general," she answered in an equally low voice.

"What are all those letters behind his name?"

"Queen's Counsel, Order of the British Empire, Master of Arts."

He sounded important. We read the letter:

My Dear Solicitor Collymore:

I pray that this unpleasant request that I make will not interfere with far more important duties. However, I ask your able assistance in apprehending a young girl named Wendy Lynn Appleton, British subject and resident of London, whom I believe was foolishly persuaded to take passage on the American bark Christine Conyers, *due to arrive shortly in Bridgetown.*

For almost six months, I have attempted to return this thirteen-year-old child to England and have been thwarted continuously by ignorant people residing in a desolate village on the North Carolina Outer Banks, principally one Benjamin O'Neal, known to have signed on as a crew member of the Conyers.

Briefly, I had Miss Appleton in my personal custody last month and had made arrangements for her return passage. An incorrigible child, she refused to abide by certain normal procedures and ran away, along with a dog. Within a few days, the O'Neal boy visited my office and I had suspicion he was involved. With whereabouts of the girl still unknown, I spent two days checking crew lists of departing vessels and discovered that young O'Neal had indeed joined the Conyers. Logic guided me to the belief that he had somehow stowed her away on that vessel.

I respectfully request that you meet the Conyers and investigate. Should the Appleton girl be aboard, I would deeply appreciate it if you would return her here to me in Norfolk on the first available British-flag ship. Further, the O'Neal boy should be informed that any untoward steps that he takes will result in immediate arrest for interference with legal proceedings of a sovereign nation.

Insofar as the dog is concerned, should it be accompanying the girl, I would suggest you shoot it and toss it on a refuse pile, where it belongs.

I trust and hope that you are in good health and enjoying your office on that beautiful island with our fellow countrymen. I envy you.

Most sincerely,
Henry Calderham
Her Majesty's Consul-General
Norfolk, Virginia
USA

Never in my life had I read such a mean letter. I would have given anything for Cousin Filene to be standing in that cabin with us as Tee passed it back, shaking and helpless. Had I been able to get in touch with Heron Head station, every Banker over twelve would be packing his kit for the Barbadoes.

Cap'n Reddy broke the awful silence by saying to Tee, "I'm sorry. There's nothing I can do. I did inform Mr. Collymore that you were not a stowaway."

Tee swallowed and nodded, seeming to shrink.

It had been kind of a lark for her to come aboard the *Conyers*, but she'd meant well. Now, send her back under arrest? Shoot Boo? Not by a ton of snakes, I thought, getting mad. What I couldn't figure out was how Calderham's short arm had reached so far in so short a time.

I asked Queen's Counsel Collymore. "How did that letter get here so fast?"

"Not that it's any of your business, the *Cashamara* brought it in a week ago," he said, and in almost the same breath, "Now, young lady, gather your things."

The coal-burning, steam-spouting *Cashamara*. Modern conveniences.

Tee got enough possession of herself to ask, "Is Lord Footman on the island?"

Collymore answered, "His Excellency is on holiday in England. Now, please gather your things."

Tee's face dropped again.

I had a scant moment with the victim of the Empire's officials while she was packing her kit: the clothes Mama had made or bought for her, several dresses and a pair of shoes that she'd acquired in Norfolk on that shopping trip with Calderham.

"Why did you want to know about that Lord Footman? Who is he?" I asked.

"The Governor-General. He knew my father, and also likes dogs. He has a fine basset hound named King Pellinore."

She was throwing her things around. The shock had worn off, and Tee was riled now, I could see. From past experience, I knew she could get riled as well as stubborn. Little lines of fiery red were around her lips.

"Ben," she said, "I am not going to England

without Boo. That's very definite, no matter all the police on earth."

I tried to calm her down. "There's nothing we can do now," I said in a fatherly tone. "Best you go on, and I'll try to find a way to get him over there. As soon as I get back to Norfolk. I'll try to find a ship that will take him. I promise."

Tee shook her head defiantly. "Where I go, Boo goes."

I said, "Don't worry about anyone shooting him. I don't think there's a man on this ship, even the bosun, who'd let that happen."

Tee finished stuffing her things into the cardboard case and whirled around. "I know this island better than that silly solicitor. Ben, tomorrow you meet me at Cole's Cave, in St. Thomas Parish, and bring Boo with you."

Not that! "Tee, you can't run away again," I pleaded.

"I certainly can, and will," she said flatly. "You meet me, Ben. Don't you fail. Go up the beach road to Holetown, this side of Six Men's Bay and Speightstown, then go inland. The cave's on a plantation, not too far from Dunscombe and Welchman Hall. Ask anybody."

I was about to ask, *And then what do we do?* when Sergeant Watkins poked his ebony head into the cabin. "I say, are you ready?"

Tee replied, "Quite, officer."

Along with Boo, I followed them up the companionway and out onto deck, where Cap'n Reddy and the solicitor awaited. Dry-eyed and grim, Tee said good-bye to the captain, to me, and to Boo, and then turned to Collymore. "I'll do what's right, sir," she said.

Now, that had a very familiar ring, straight from the Widow O'Neal, and I thought to myself, *Well, here we go again.* Everybody would be wise to hang on to their straps.

Tee waved farewell as the Lord Nelson oarsmen shoved off and headed for the Queen's Dock.

Boo let out a moan, though he had no idea what was going on. Simply, Calderham had succeeded in splitting the Rock of Gibraltar, after all.

Cap'n Reddy observed, "She's quite a girl."

Few could deny that, one way or another.

20

"VELL, VAS ISS DIS all about now?" the bosun was asking in his usual frightening roar as the Harbour Police skiff rounded the jetty and disappeared into the busy basin. He hadn't heard.

With heavy heart, I told him.

He eyed Bridgetown with alarm and said, as if personally insulted, "Dey can't do dat." Like practically everyone, except officials like Calderham and Collymore, the bosun had grown fond of the castaway girl. "If de *Fräulein* vants her *Hund,* den she should have her *Hund.*" He reached down and gave Boo a flat-hand pat on the head, surprising both the dog and myself.

"I think so, too," I said, seeing a sudden, unexpected ray of hope.

"Vell, vas iss she goin' to do?" he asked.

Truth was wisest, so I said, "She's going to run away and hide in a cave. She knows how, all right. I'm supposed to meet her tomorrow with Boo."

The bosun, frowning toward the port, said, "*Ach,* das iss no way to do it. She'll never get off de land, much less mitt *das Hund.*"

"What's more," I warned, "they may shoot Boo if he goes ashore."

"*Nein,*" Gebbert growled. *No,* it meant, I had learned from less pleasant experiences.

"That's what the letter said."

"Den he stays safe here," said Gebbert, looking thoughtfully around at other ships in the anchorage, as if he had an idea.

I could now see much more than a ray of hope. With the bosun on our side, the whole late-afternoon sky was filled with it. Gebbert alone was equal to about twenty Collymores, fifty Calderhams, and a few of the West Indies Regiment. I only wished there was some way to get word to Tee to sit tight.

Finally the bosun said, "Tell you vas; after supper I'll take a *Boot und* make some of dese ships. Ve'll get her back mitt *das Hund*."

"What will the cap'n say?" I asked, now worried about him. "He told her he couldn't help."

The bosun said, "De cap'n will help. He don't like officials, but he likes de *Fräulein*."

In about an hour, word was all over the *Conyers* about Teetoncey's latest plight, and no less than six sailors, including Nils and Barney and the Bravaman, offered assistance. I said the bosun was taking care of it for the time being, and they decided to let well enough alone. Eddie Cartaxo was right: In time of trouble, Gebbert was the one.

By supper, the captain and the second mate were ashore. The bosun and the chief mate ate their meals pretty much in silence, and then Gebbert left the saloon, saying to me, "Ve'll see now."

I went up on deck as he hailed a boat to begin making the rounds of all the American ships in

Carlisle Bay. There were two steamers, a bark, and two big schooners.

In the galley, I asked Eddie where they might be keeping Tee ashore, still having thoughts of trying to contact her, telling her to make no moves until we could work it out. "Probably in an inn," the Bravaman said. "I don't think they'd put her in Graystone."

I asked what Graystone was.

"Graystone Gaol, the old jail. It's a very bad place. I've stayed there under lock and key. So has the bosun; even the cap'n, a long time ago when he drank a lot."

"Hans is trying to help," I said.

Eddie laughed. "You see, I told you."

"He doesn't seem to like the police here."

Eddie laughed once more. "That's because of Graystone. One night he wiped out half of the Ice House—that's a famous saloon over there—when a British sailor called him an ugly swine. He must have decked twenty men before someone threw a table at him and knocked him off the second-floor balcony. After a week in jail, the bosun came back half starved and full of lice. So he doesn't like Graystone.

"I don't think the girl is there," Eddie added.

At soft twilight, tide incoming, all ships riding easy at anchor, I sat on the stern of the *Conyers* with Boo, looking at the lamp and lantern lights of Bridgetown, hearing voices and laughter and music. It was awful. *My first foreign port. My first night in the tropics.* I said to Boo, "Wouldn't you know we'd end up here instead of walking around Trafalgar Square and eating fish pie?" It seemed to me that we were both doomed until we got that girl safely back to London.

I sat out there a long time, just thinking, and, about nine o'clock, a skiff made the accommodation ladder and I ran back just in time to see the bosun climb up. I was close enough to get a good whiff of rum or whiskey, not that it mattered. So he had been tippling a bit after a long, hard voyage, seeing old friends. What was wrong with that?

He eyed me and said, "Vee did it. See dat four-mastered schooner out dere . . ."

I couldn't see anything except some yellow anchor lights, and that didn't matter, either.

The bosun said, "De *Fräulein und* de *Hund* sail in two days. She goes to Baltimore."

Spirits soaring, I asked, "How did you do it?"

He laughed and waved a hand as if it were nothing. "Vee did it," he repeated, and weaved on toward the afterhouse companionway.

I knew better than to press him. Details could wait for the morrow. And Baltimore was as good a place as any, providing Tee avoided the criminal element.

I returned to the stern again to watch and listen to Bridgetown. A singing voice floated out over the water:

"Darlin', your man's got to stay on shore
  Those tall, white sails don't fly no more . . .

[Not so, I thought.]

"Small island, small island, you've gone back
    on your wish
  Small island, tell the waves to come on shore

My ship is rottin' in the slip, go tell the flyin'
  fish
This sailor won't be out to sea no more . . ."

[Not me, I thought.]

My mind was very much on the girl. She was over there, lonely and worried, mourning Boo, probably in an inn, police guard outside the door. I couldn't think of anything worse.

Boo snored gently beside me in the velvet night, enjoying the cool breeze, as I thought on, even to the point that we O'Neals had surely been selected to pilot Teetoncey all the way home. Since the night she'd washed up into our hands, the Mother Sea had decreed that we would be responsible. Soon I decided it was nothing less than a holy mission to personally get that girl to London. That being the case, it was I, Ben O'Neal, who must escort her every ocean mile.

Therefore I was duty-bound to be on that schooner when it sailed.

The shore sounds began to ebb, and the lights began to fade away about ten o'clock. Then I saw the cap'n and second mate return, likely having had broiled flying fish topped with creole sauce. Several other skiffs made the accommodation ladder shortly after that, bearing tipsy crew members. They were laughing and talking loudly, and I stayed in the shadows.

Finally I went on down to the pantry with Boo and turned in, knowing that dawn would begin an interesting day.

21

THE CREW TURNED-TO about six-thirty of that beautiful morning to open No. 2 hatch and begin off-loading the small amount of general cargo destined for Bridgetown. Lighters were already alongside to begin hauling the short distance back to the docks.

I began serving breakfast about seven o'clock, as usual, trying to stay in the pantry while the bosun talked to the captain about Tee, not wanting to interfere at this point. No sooner had the cap'n and the bosun finished their pancakes and a second cup of coffee than I was instructed to summon the Bravaman aft. The captain, now rightfully performing in his true role, had taken charge, and I ran up the deck to get Eddie Cartaxo.

The conference that then took place was of even more importance than the meeting we'd held with the railroaders in Mrs. Crowe's parlor, amid the ferns. There was no nonsense or fiddle-faddling about it.

Cap'n Reddy began by saying he'd never been involved in anything like this in his forty-six years at sea, but neither had the rest of us, no matter how long we'd sailed. Then he spoke directly to the Bravaman. "Eddie, you take Ben and go ashore to do your usual shopping [the buying of fresh vegetables and fruit for the galley], but find the girl first and take her out to the beach at Holetown. Hans will go there in the yawl and bring her back to the *Ritter*."

It was not until that moment that I knew the name of the schooner that would carry Tee on to Baltimore. I had not spoken but felt I must now. "Cap'n, please let me go with her. That girl needs someone to look out for her all the way."

Josiah Reddy regarded me for a moment, then nodded. "That was on my mind, too. If Eddie can find someone to replace you, I'll sign you off and you can sail with Cap'n Tobias." Then he added to the Bravaman, "Ask around at Da Costa's."

Eddie replied confidently, "We'll find some-one."

I cannot describe the relief I felt, and said so gratefully, then took the five companionway rungs at almost one leap to go out on deck. About six hundred yards away, gray-hulled, with white rail-ings, white deckhouses, white mastheads and trucks, *Harriet B. Ritter* swung at anchor in the calm water, taking on the last of her load of sugar. I'd noticed the trim four-master the previ-ous day but little dreamt I'd ever set foot on her.

Two hours later, the Bravaman, with a tarpau-lin folded beneath his arm, hailed a boat, and we went shoreward toward the jetty on sparkling-clear water. I had no idea what the tarp was for but looked back at the *Conyers* and saw the bosun, along with Nils, preparing to launch the yawl. The plan of action was under way.

Within a few minutes, we rounded the jetty and there was the bustling port of Bridgetown, and the Careenage, gem of the Caribbees, jammed with two-masted Indies schooners and dozens of little cargo barges. In the Careenage, several schooners were tilted over, their masts pulled toward rings on the quay, their bottoms almost out of the water. Men were caulking and painting.

Our boat bumped up against the dock not far from where a hand derrick was lowering bags of sugar into the lighters. Nearby, workmen were tightening hoops on barrels of molasses, freight for some ship. Wherever I looked, cargo was being hand-loaded into the interisland schooners, brought up by low-slung, two-wheeled donkey carts.

That morning was like most mornings in the Lesser Antilles, warm and soft, with wind rustling the palms and fleecy clouds racing overhead. There was a thick, sweet smell in the air, maybe from all the sugarcane and tropical plants.

The Harbour Police on the dock eyed us but

said nothing, and I could only guess that Tee hadn't as yet escaped. If she had, they knew nothing about it. We went about our business, which was to go to Da Costa's.

Looking about, I was almost speechless but asked Eddie, as we passed one loading schooner, the *Jeannie Johnson,* of Castries, "Where do you think that one will go?" Whatever cargo was down in her hold, on her deck were bags of fertilizer, sacks of cement, rolls of wire, kegs of nails, and some live pigs. Passengers sat on her rails to await departure.

"Oh, maybe Dominica; then back to her home, Saint Lucy. She'll return with firewood, grapefruit, mangoes, chickens. Anything. That's how everyone gets around down here."

I saw stone warehouses that must have dated back to George Washington's famous visit, in 1751. Lookout towers to spot incoming ships mounted up from several warehouses. Then I saw the bridges, seven of them, after which the town is named, connecting all the basins. In the air now was another smell: food cooking. Noisy hum was cut through by the cries of vendors.

"Fish hey. Fish hey."

"Dolphin. Dolphin."

"Nuseful limes. Nuseful limes."

Then one that stood over all: "Maubey cooo-ooool! Maubey cooo-oo-ool!"

We crossed Chamberlain Bridge, over the Careenage, and there was Trafalgar Square, with the tall Lord Nelson statue, just as Tee had said. Not ten paces off that bridge was a towering, bearded man wrapped in a silk sheet, with more silk wound around his head, sandals on his feet, beads hanging down from his neck, like no man I'd ever seen. I'm afraid I gawked.

"Hindu," Eddie said. "A few here. Some Moslems, too. Few Bengalese. Few Chinese. Quite a few Portuguese."

It was all more than two eyes could ever take in and one brain ever think about.

As we moved along Broad Street at the Bravaman's limp speed, there were vendors on every corner sitting by baskets of fruit or vegetables, calling to us. Eddie waved and smiled at them. One man had some white, spiny things laid out on canvas. "Sea eggs," said Eddie. "White urchins. Very good. The meat inside is orange-coral."

In a moment, I heard the cry of "Maubey cooo-oo-oool!" again and saw a woman with a keg on her head. In front of it was a tap. The keg looked too heavy to be sitting up there. Her skin was golden brown.

"Maubey seller," said Eddie. "Look at her neck. It could hold the bridge up. You'll like this drink. Made from the bark of the maubey tree."

We stopped and Eddie paid a penny each for two tin cups of it. The woman reached up easily, balancing the big keg on the top of her head; turned the tap, and the cool drink flowed down. She caught it without spilling a drop.

Moving on, the Bravaman said, "She was mixed-blood, creole, but Bajan, too. All the Barbadians, except the whites, call themselves Bajans. Some are black as our galley coal. Some like the maubey woman. Some in between, like me."

"Why does she carry that keg on her head?" I asked.

Eddie laughed. "So she can keep her hands free. My Delfina, back in Brava, can go down the road with a bundle of wood on her head and still crochet; never miss a loop."

All this time, I scarcely thought of Tee, and one could hardly blame me. Here I was in Bridgetown, with wind bending the palm trees, and Bajans and Hindus, and foods of which I'd never heard; sights I'd never seen. Reuben hadn't told me the half of it.

At the corner of Broad and MacGregor, I saw the Ice House saloon, a three-story building with a balcony running around the second floor, the undoing of Bosun Gebbert. I did not see Graystone Gaol and had no desire to do so.

Then we turned into Da Costa's, and it reminded me, just a little bit, of Jordan's. Captains were sitting around drinking rum. A big board listed all the companies Da Costa handled: PACIFIC ARGENTINE BRAZIL; WEST AFRICAN LIGHTERAGE & TRANSPORT COMPANY, LIVERPOOL; SKIBS A/S HOSANGER, BERGEN, NORWAY. Many more.

"Captains come in here to get cargoes," said

Eddie. "Or just to pass time while loading or unloading."

Then the Bravaman began spouting Portuguese to a clerk. They talked quite a while, and then Eddie turned to say, "He'll have someone for us by tonight."

That was good news. I could now sail on the *Ritter.*

After he borrowed a lantern, which we'd forgotten, there was another long rattle of Portuguese. Finally Eddie said, *"Adeus,"* waved his hand good-bye, and we were off again.

"What was all that last talk about?" I asked.

"We talked about how nice it would be to have some *carne de porco à alentejana* for dinner."

I frowned.

"Pork with clams. But I told him I had an important job to do." That was rescue Tee, of course, from Cole's Cave, trusting that she was there.

In a moment, Eddie hired a Bajan cart named Daily Bread and its driver, Arthur Cobes. Eddie used him each time the *Conyers* came to the Barbadoes. I hopped in back, where the Bravaman had thrown the tarpaulin, and we started off for Holetown.

Eddie talked in his *j*'s that sounded like *s*'s and *g*'s and was answered back in a flow of warm Bajan syrup. Eddie asked how Mrs. Cobes was, and her husband answered, "Ah, we gettin' on in a certain way," which wasn't much of an answer. Then they fell to talking about mango crabs. A crab is a crab, whether in Barbadoes or up to Manteo. So the topic didn't hold much interest for me.

I looked at the countryside, seeing all the tropical vegetation. Carts loaded with sugarcane and yams passed us going in the opposite direction. The road was a little like our sand trails on the Banks, but the countryside wasn't. Sugar mills were everywhere.

Soon the Daily Bread cut back toward the sea, and the beaches could be seen again, white and pink. The sand looked powdery, and I'd never had sky like this overhead. For some reason, it was a different shade of blue from the Hatteras sky; the clouds were different. They were lower and moved faster. The palm trees were flapping a music. The heat was moist.

Only once during that enjoyable ride did Eddie talk to me. He looked behind us and said, "No police are following." Mind a million miles away, I'd forgotten all about Collymore and his threats.

We turned sharp right in Holetown, which wasn't much of a place, and went east into the rolling lands of St. Thomas Parish. Everywhere along the road were pieces of sugarcane, dropped during the harvest season. Some was still being cut. The cream-colored donkey pulling us along now had his work cut out, as we were steadily going upward.

Mr. Cobes knew exactly where that Cole's Cave was, on the Spring Plantation. Caves do not exist on the Outer Banks, to my knowledge, probably due to the high sand content, and I was looking forward to seeing one, in addition to finding Tee. She certainly picked unusual places to hide.

In little more than an hour, we arrived at the brink of a steep ravine and Arthur Cobes said, "Down there."

We all got off and started descending into the ravine and finally reached the cave entrance. It was a shaft, which Mr. Cobes called a "suc," which did not register with me. I looked into the stony darkness and called out for Tee. An echo came back just like the ones on the stairwell of Hatteras Light. There was no answer.

The Bravaman lit the lantern and said, "We'll take a look."

I quickly discovered that I do not like caves. Although it was warm in there and we could hear water running, I was not attracted to the bats that were hanging to the high ceiling once we got into the main part. Nor did I like the looks of the dripping stone icicles that hung down, with others rising from the floor, appearing to try to kiss.

I kept calling for Tee, now believing that she hadn't made it. But in a moment there was an answer back, and we rounded another area and there she was, sitting on a bedsheet. She'd been asleep.

She hopped up and said, "I knew you'd come," and then said hello to the Bravaman and Mr. Cobes.

Right away, she asked about Boo, and I told her he was safe aboard the *Conyers;* they'd be united presently. Then I said, "Let's get out of here."

"It's really a good place to sleep, Ben. It's so warm, and you can hear the water running."

"Do you know there are bats in here?" I asked.

"Certainly I do. I've come here many times."

We went on out, and that was my first and last visit to a cave. I just do not like them.

Climbing back up, we got into the cart and I discovered why Eddie had brought the tarpaulin along. He threw it over us, and we started downhill again for Holetown. As we bumped along the trail, Eddie and Cobes talking upon the seat, I asked Tee, "How long were you in that cave?"

"I got there about two o'clock this morning."

"Were you in jail or an inn?"

"No, I was in Collymore's home," she said. "He lives on Bathsheba Road, not far from Codrington College."

"How'd you get away?"

She laughed. "For a Solicitor-General, he isn't very smart. I talked to his housekeeper, and told her what they'd done to me, and why. Just after dark, she rode a donkey down to our former plantation in Christ Church and told Mr. Littlefield, our foreman, what had happened to me. They are both Bajan and very understanding people."

"Collymore's own housekeeper betrayed him?"

She nodded.

I think the lesson to be learned by Calderham and Collymore was that you did not pick on female orphans, rich or poor, nor their dogs.

"Then what happened?" I asked.

"Well, I put a note on my door for Collymore saying, 'I'm very tired, please do not disturb me,' then crawled out of the window about midnight, when everyone was asleep. Mr. Littlefield met me on Bathsheba Road on his horse and off we went. I'm sure Collymore was surprised this morning."

"I'm sure he was," I said, quickly recalling the notes she'd left Mrs. Crowe and myself on the dining table.

It was very hot under that piece of canvas and I was sweating all over. That part of the ride wasn't so nice, and Tee brought up another point. "You're not seeing much of Barbados, are you?"

No, I wasn't, actually, especially under that tarpaulin. I had wanted to see those Scotch Redleg slaves and the cannon on the beach at Speightstown; that regimental signal tower; but now I knew those sights would have to await another voyage. At that, I was faring better than Boo. Here he was in his first foreign port and hadn't been able to lift a single leg ashore.

It was well past noon when we arrived on the powdery, pink beach at Holetown, and there, as planned, were the bosun and Nils. The bosun greeted Tee happily, saying, *"Guten Tag,"* which means good afternoon, and they jabbered in German for a moment; then she climbed into the yawl, ducked down, and Gebbert shoved off, quickly raising sail. He made a long tack and then headed east for Carlisle Bay and the schooner *Ritter*.

So far, so good.

We went back to Bridgetown the same way we'd come and I was relieved to be out from under the sticky heat of the tarp.

We went directly to a market on a narrow street called Swan, and there Eddie bought bananas, plums, sweetsop (a pulpy fruit I'd never seen before), pawpaw (a smaller, orange-colored fruit, also new to me), yams, string beans, carrots, cabbage, and beets. Tossing the tarpaulin over them, we made our way back to the dock.

Just before we got there, Mr. Cobes, looking ahead, suddenly said, very quietly, "Bruggadung." I learned later that it is supposed to be said very loudly, *BRUGGADUNG*, and means two forces colliding with bad results. On the dock was the Queen's Solicitor, Sergeant Watkins, and about a half dozen police.

We plodded on out there in the Daily Bread, and Collymore came at almost a run to jerk the canvas cover off the vegetables. "Where is the girl?" he demanded.

"Isn't she in Graystone Gaol?" I answered.

He was furious. "No, she ran away last night. She left a note on her door saying she was tired, and I didn't check until almost noon today."

Tee was right. He wasn't very smart.

The Bravaman shook his head. "We haven't seen her lately." And that was true. It had been more than an hour since we'd left Holetown.

Mr. Cobes offered his advice with a gleeful grin. "M'lud, mebbe she lick-about the caves."

Collymore threw him an angry glare, and we began unloading the vegetables as the Queen's Counsel, now irate, shouted to search all the schooners in the basin. The poor, completely innocent *Jeannie Johnson,* of Castries, was boarded a moment later by six police, setting off pig squeals.

Soon I bade Bridgetown farewell, having only seen a bit of it. Both ships would sail at the dawning Friday, April 7.

22

About five-thirty, when I was beginning to carry supper aft, three Harbour Police boats, loaded to the gunwales, rounded the jetty and dipped oars toward the *Christine Conyers*. In the lead boat was the Queen's Solicitor, standing like an explorer. In a few minutes, Basil Collymore, Sergeant Watkins, and six or seven more of Her Majesty's police came up the accommodation ladder. Called to deck, Cap'n Reddy greeted Solicitor Collymore warmly. "Welcome back to the *Conyers*," he said, unafraid of the official.

Collymore's starchy reply was, "I really doubt if I'm welcome. The Appleton girl disappeared from my home last night and we're here to search the vessel. I have the proper papers, Captain."

Josiah Reddy smiled. He was not the least bit awed. "You don't need papers for that. Look as you might."

"Where is that dog?" Collymore asked suspiciously.

With two fingers between my teeth, I let loose a blast. Old Boo came trotting out from behind the afterhouse, tail wagging, grinning at Collymore, it seemed to me, leathers black and shiny. A nasty grin, almost.

Satisfied about that, Collymore nodded unhappily and then ordered Sergeant Watkins to search the ship. Some of the police went forward, some aft, and all hands just stood by aloofly for about twenty minutes. The police poked through the crew's quarters and galley, down into the forward hatch. They looked around the afterhouse and finally gave up.

Cap'n Reddy said to Collymore, "You see, she isn't aboard."

The solicitor replied doggedly, "We'll find her, sir. The island's too small to hide her."

Cap'n Reddy agreed. "That seems to be a fair statement."

Solicitor Collymore was first down the ladder into the boats, and Sergeant Watkins was last. Just before he set foot on the immaculate wooden grillwork of the platform, Watkins said to Cap'n Reddy, "The little girl isn't on this ship, is she?"

"Of course not," the captain replied.

The sergeant then looked down at the runty figure of Collymore Q.C., O.B.E., M.A. with great disdain and smiled, his teeth sparkling against his black skin. "But she is on a ship?"

"I wouldn't be surprised," the captain answered soberly.

Sergeant Watkins said, "I hope she has a safe voyage home," saluted smartly, and then pounded on down the accommodation ladder.

We watched them go, knowing that Tee was now as safe as Boo's fleas, quoting Mama. Everyone was helping, and as night edged across Carlisle Bay and Bridgetown, I packed my seabag for transfer to the *Harriet B. Ritter*. Then, in late evening, I said my good-byes and gratitudes to Cap'n Reddy, Eddie Cartaxo, Bosun Gebbert, Nils, and Barney, some of the finest men who ever walked a deck.

It pays to have foreign-speaking friends, as I learned about eleven o'clock that night when a boat bearing Boo and myself bumped against the *Ritter*'s ladder. A sleepy sailor was on gangway and anchor watch; Tee was on hand, of course, to greet her four-footed lover. They were happily rejoined on the midships deck of that sleeping schooner beneath a tropic quarter moon. Bridgetown, across the way, was quiet and lifeless.

Tee said, "Oh, Ben, I'm so glad to see you," as if we hadn't fried under the tarp in the afternoon. But she lavished most of her attention on Boo, as expected.

I still did not know how Hans Gebbert had worked all this out and promptly asked. Tee said it was very simple. The chief mate of the *Ritter* had been born in a place called Wilhelmshaven. So it was that two sentimental Germans had put their heads together to rescue the British castaway girl. And that's why Gebbert had said to me, "Vee did it." The two of them. They struck a blow against the Collymores and Graystone Gaol.

However, I had been very instrumental myself in putting the whole thing together and expected some praise. I did not get it. She jabbered on about the two Germans, and my feelings were a little bit hurt. I finally said, "Tee, it's been a long day and I probably have to work tomorrow."

She replied, "Yes, you do. Gustav said he would use you in the crew."

So it was "Gustav" already for the chief mate, first-name basis, and undoubtedly they had jabbered back and forth at each other, courtesy of the teaching of Tee's cook back in London. I repeat that it pays to know a foreign language, but Tee seemed to make friends easily in any language.

"Crew? I'm glad to hear that," I said. No more being a waiter, washing dishes; scrubbing the captain's bathtub. "They have a galley boy on here?"

"A galleyman," she corrected. "Your exact position will be as a workaway."

That meant I wouldn't get paid. I didn't mind that so much, but I was suddenly annoyed—coming aboard my second ship and having her know everything about it. Whether she knew it or not, she was acting like Kilbie Oden back on the Banks, this warm late night. Ten minutes into anything and he was an expert. Tee had now been aboard seven hours or so. "You've met the cap'n?"

She nodded. "We had dinner together. He's very nice, Ben. Nothing like Captain Reddy; he's quiet and businesslike. I told him all about you."

"What did he say?"

"Nothing."

That let me down a little more, and I said, "I think I'll go on to bed."

"Yes," she said, "find yourself a bunk in the fo'c'sle."

I stared at her in the moonglow. *The fo'c'sle.* She was beginning to get very nautical. I was tempted to ask if she'd taken over the bosun's job. Instead I said, "That's where the crew usually sleeps."

She yawned and scruffed Boo's neck. "We'll go along, Ben. The hatches have all been caulked. Everything is ready. We sail at dawn."

Just like Kilbie, and I ignored it. "Where are you two sleeping?"

"We have a spacious cabin aft. It even has a freshwater basin in it. And the captain told me that anytime I wanted to take a bath, please use his tub. I'm afraid you're restricted to one bucket of freshwater a week. You'll have to use seawater other times."

That didn't matter. Oh, was I glad I wouldn't be galley-swamper on this voyage. Scrubbing her bathtub ring would be the final undoing.

She smiled at me in the Caribbee silver light and leaned forward and upward to kiss my forehead. "I'm so glad you're aboard, Ben," she said, and bid me good night.

I grunted the same as she disappeared toward the companionway of the afterhouse, hound padding beside her, joyously reunited. Like Mama,

Filene, Jabez, and so many other Bankers before them, I believe that I was acquiring the knowledge to take things in stride. My main goal was to deliver that girl back in England and I could not let petty things stand in the way.

It was hot and dark inside that fo'c'sle and didn't smell very good, but I found an empty bunk among the eight. The snores inside that cabin were enough to saw the *Ritter's* oak keel half in two. Too tired to do anything else, I didn't bother to undress, just took my shoes off and crawled upon that *donkey's breakfast,* finding it just as lumpy and moldy as the one on the *Conyers.* The night passed. Quickly, it seemed to me.

Suddenly there were noise and talking. A lamp had been lighted, and all around the cabin men were pulling on their trousers and shirts, slipping their galluses over their shoulders; cinching their belts. Scratching and groaning, they paid little attention to me.

I threw my legs over the bunk, got on my shoes, and stumbled around a minute, waited my turn at the crew's toilet, washed my face and hands in seawater, then had coffee and a biscuit, introducing myself to whoever was interested.

Eventually the bosun came forward for coffee and saw me. His name was Malone, and he was old and leathery. He said, "Stand by the bow, and hose the anchor chain when we get under way. Keep your feet out of the running gear."

I said, "Yessir."

Malone said, "I'm not a 'sir,'" and that was that.

Smoke drifted up from the stacks of the donkey-engine boilers on both ships at cool, reddish dawn. Spouts of steam were coming out forward from both the *Conyers* and the *Ritter,* and the slow clank of windlass pawls broke the bay silence as anchor chain came aboard. I squirted ours, though there wasn't any mud on it, Carlisle Bay having a sand bottom.

Soon, puffs of gray began to stand out on the *Conyers* as she raised sail, even as the anchor was heaving in. Then I heard Frank, the chanteyman, begin "Away to Rio," and knew exactly what was happening on the deck of the bark, Cap'n Josiah Reddy standing aft like a sea god. For them Brazil was almost a month away. For a few seconds, I felt a chill going up and down my spine. I felt a sadness, too.

Several of the *Ritter* sailors laughed when they heard the chantey. Fools they were, I thought. They were already spoiled with modern conveniences. They did not have salt in their blood.

Neither was Cap'n Tobias old-fashioned like Cap'n Reddy. He would have nothing to do with ancient chanteys and such. Tall and thin, with sparse white hair, a brush of milky mustache, gaunt-faced, he was wearing white pants, a white shirt, and a blue felt squash cap. Not much different from the Manteo lawyer who judged the sharpie races on July Fourth in Shallowbag Bay.

The sails on the *Ritter* would be mostly raised by the steam engine, not hand-hauled. The halyards would be led forward to the gypsyheads, steel drums on either side of the fo'c'sle house. The gasping engine would do the work of pulling canvas up. Far cry from the glorious *Conyers*.

Soon the captain walked forward, looked around, and said quietly to the mate, "Set the mizzen." Nothing like a rousing Reddy yell. And the throat and peak halyards were quickly led to the gypsyheads. In a moment "Gustav" said, as if still half asleep, "Heave away togedder." It was all humdrum compared to the *Conyers.*

Tee and Boo came up about that time, and I said a depressed good morning as I went about my squirting. They stood out of the way, near the fo'c'sle.

After the anchor came up short, chain almost straight down, the *Ritter*'s mains'il was set, as was the fores'il; then the jibs. Finally "Gustav" called out tiredly, "Man to the wheel," and then the anchor was heaved home. The four-master *Harriet B. Ritter* paid off before the wind.

As the anchor chain was stopped off for sea and the hose went limp, I looked longingly at the *Conyers,* still hearing a faint "Up she rises" as the bark, too, took the breeze and got under way for Rio, fleeting and fluttering like a giant bird, enough to take a person's breath away.

I had just a moment to stand by Tee and Boo. I said, "Oh, my, there goes a grand vessel, Tee." She nodded. I even think Boo felt the same. We were all of blue mood.

So the two ships went their separate courses, on separate tacks. Cap'n Reddy looping out for the southeast; Cap'n Tobias to haul around and slide between St. Vincent and St. Lucia, headed for Mona Passage, up off Porto Rico, north-bound.

As workaway, I polished brasswork, tarred the rigging, painted a little now and then, and stood the 8-to-12 P.M. lookout watch on the bow; helped change sail now and then during the sixteen-day trip.

There isn't much to tell about that voyage north. As workers, the sailors were no better or worse than those on the *Conyers*, but they seemed dull as oyster hulls in comparison to Cap'n Reddy, the Bravaman, and Bosun Gebbert.

The weather was mostly good, and I worked away as best I could. Tee did her usual, captivating everyone on the ship. Compared to her and that dog, I was just tolerated. I suffered silently, keeping my goal in mind. I did convince Tee that we three should get off in Norfolk, and she twisted Cap'n Tobias and "Gustav" around her finger to accomplish that.

On April 21, we were put ashore in the pilot boat as the *Harriet B. Ritter* continued her voyage to Baltimore.

23

AFTER A LONG WALK from the pilot station, we were on the front porch of Mrs. Crowe's about 3:30 P.M., and I rang her bell. In a moment, the door opened and she stood there, mouth agape. She said, "I never thought you'd come back here." Yet I noticed that she didn't seem surprised that Tee and the dog were still in my tow.

"You've been all over the newspapers," she said.

We had? That stunned me.

"We've only been to the Barbadoes island," I said.

"And you escaped handily from there, the *Pilot* said day before yesterday."

I didn't like the way she used the word "escaped." Nor did I like the fact that she seemed very nervous, as if she preferred we go quickly away. She didn't invite us in. I said, "We came back on another ship. The British authorities tried to arrest Tee."

Mrs. Crowe nodded. "It's been all over the paper."

Be that as it may I said, "Mrs. Crowe, we'd like to rent two rooms for several nights and straighten out our problems; keep Boo down in the basement."

She seemed very jumpy, not at all like her old, spicy self. "Well, I don't know, Ben. I could get in trouble with the city, even the federal government. I've never harbored fugitives before. Knowingly, anyway."

"Fugitives?" I echoed, in a shocked tone. "You know we haven't done anything wrong."

"That's not what the British consul told the *Pilot*. I've got those stories inside. And you didn't tell me the authorities were looking for 'Wendy Lynn Appleton' last month. That was deceitful."

Tee spoke up and told the truth: "I thought it best not to. I was only going to be here that one night."

Mrs. Crowe shook her head in dismay. "I don't know what to do. You two should really turn yourselves in."

I said to Tee, "Maybe we should talk about that." It was all far more serious than I ever thought. The newspapers, of all things. I'd never even been in the Manteo weekly, except as next of kin to John and Rachel O'Neal. And now that I had made it, it was probably as a criminal.

Mrs. Crowe looked up and down the street, then said, with misgiving, "Well, come on in and we'll talk. But I make no promises."

So we went in, and I took Boo down to the basement, then returned to the parlor. Mrs. Crowe was still jumpy and promptly brought out two clippings.

The first one was from March and reported that Consul Calderham had alerted Norfolk police to a British runaway, further stating that he believed this juvenile, Wendy Lynn Appleton by name, had been persuaded to stow away on a Brazil-bound ship by thirteen-year-old Benjamin O'Neal, of Heron Head, North Carolina. Further stated was that O'Neal and others of Heron Head had repeatedly thwarted the efforts of Consul Calderham to return the girl to London.

It was nothing but a repeat of the mean letter to Collymore, and I quickly pointed out to Mrs. Crowe that Calderham had not told the *Pilot* the reason *why* Tee had run away in the first place: the reason the landlady well knew, down in the basement at this point. But I noticed that Mrs. Crowe began to ease her nerves a bit.

Then we read the second clipping dated two days previous, and I submit it here:

RUNAWAYS EVADE BRITISH POLICE ON BARBADOS

Two juveniles sought by the Norfolk police were reported today to have evaded British authorities on the island of Barbados several weeks ago.

British Consul General Henry Calderham

said that he had received a letter from the Honorable Basil Collymore, Queen's Solicitor at Bridgetown, stating that Wendy Lynn Appleton, a British juvenile being sought for removal to her native country, had apparently escaped and was thought to be aboard an American vessel bound for Baltimore. The letter was brought to Norfolk by the Furness ship, Cashamara, arriving yesterday.

(*That swift ship again,* I thought.)

Consul Calderham said that the Appleton girl probably was still in company of the one Benjamin O'Neal, a "dodgy" Outer Banks boy believed to have aided her flight from Norfolk in March. Calderham stated that he was requesting the U.S. Marshal to issue a warrant for O'Neal's arrest and is receiving the full cooperation of United States immigration officials in apprehending the girl.

No wonder Mrs. Crowe had been nervous at the front door. We sounded worse than thieves and murderers. *Dodgy. A marshal's warrant for my arrest.* I could only imagine the dumfoundery of Filene and others on the Banks as they read this terrible story.

Sitting there in the parlor, the one person I wished was around, for many reasons, was Rachel O'Neal. Mama would never have stood for this type of official foolishness. She would have packed her kit in two minutes and come to Norfolk to face down not only Calderham but the U.S. marshal as well.

I said to Mrs. Crowe, "I have never made a telephone call in my life, but I would like to do so now. I'll pay for it." I still had nine dollars and some change of my original fund, plus two dollars and thirty cents wages from Cap'n Reddy. I could well afford a phone call.

"Who do you want to call?" Mrs. Crowe asked.

"A man named Filene Midgett at Heron Head Lifesaving Station, on the Banks."

"How can he help?" she asked.

"I'm not sure. But he doesn't think much of the British consul, and when he knows the truth about this, he may have some good advice." I further said that we Bankers were not very smart but we could use our heads together when that time came.

Mrs. Crowe thought a moment and then said, "All right, Ben, we'll call. It's long distance and you'll need to tell me how many rings so I can tell the operator here."

This was all new to me, but I did know that the station phone for Heron Head was five rings. I'd heard it enough times. So she cranked her phone around to get the operator and things began. Tee hadn't said much through all this. She seemed to be letting me take over, which I appreciated.

It took about twenty minutes, and I was praying that Filene wasn't out somewhere on his sand pony; maybe visiting Cap'n Etheridge, up to Pea Island station, or up to Chicky station to talk to the boys. Or even fishing. After all, it was April and the channel bass were running at Oregon Inlet.

Finally Mrs. Crowe said, "All right, Ben, he's coming on the telephone," and I was just as jumpy as the day I walked aboard the *Christine Conyers*. I took that hearing piece and put it up against my ear and then put my lips against the little black cone on the oak box.

I said loudly, "Cap'n Filene, this is Ben."

Immediately, my eardrum was almost broken. Then I remembered that Filene had never learned how to use a telephone properly. He shouted into it as if he were yelling for oar strokes in a wild surf. I held it away from my head.

"Ben," he thundered. "Where are you?"

"I'm in Norfolk."

"Whatta you doin' there?"

"I just got off a schooner today. I'm here with Teetoncey and Boo Dog."

It was a good thing that Filene was yelling so loud, because Mrs. Crowe and Tee could hear every word.

"Ben, the paper yestiddy sez you're in trouble. What'd you do, boy?"

Then I told him the plain, unvarnished truth. Every word of it, particularly stressing about Calderham's taking advantage of Tee once again.

I even said that the consul wanted to have Boo shot. I wound up by asking, "What should I do, Cousin?"

That phone line over miles of swamp and sand fell dead for a minute, while Filene thought. Then he came back on. "First," he shouted, "you tell that Norfawk newspaper to watch its tongue. We're good people down here and don't want no gossip spread. Second, you tell that consul, a man I don't like very much at best, to behave himself or I'll be in his office by nightfall tomorry. Third, Ben, you an' Teetoncey an' that dog turn yourselves in. Plead innocent to all charges. You got that?" Filene was always one to come through.

"Yessir," I said. "But Tee is guilty of one charge, at least. She took that thirty-one dollars. Of that fund, she still has fifteen. So she owes the British Government sixteen dollars."

Filene roared. "Don't matter that. You tell that foul Calderham we'll give him his stingy sixteen dollars for the Queen. We'll take up a collection down here an' have the Manteo bank send a draft."

I was feeling better by the moment.

"Then you come on back here where you belong an' wait for Reuben," Filene yelled.

"I can't, Keeper," I said. "I've got to get this girl safe to London. Mama would want that."

The phone line fell dead again, and I waited. "All right," he said. "Do your duty, Ben."

I thanked him for all his good advice and hung up, my palm sweaty from holding that earpiece. I blew a breath of relief on hanging it up in the cradle arm, and then turned back to Mrs. Crowe and Tee.

Right away, I could see they were encouraged, too. Filene's fighting spirit had spread all over that parlor. I said, "Tee, you heard him. That's what I think we should do. Give ourselves up."

Immediately, Mrs. Crowe was her old self again. She said, "You know, Ben, I have an idea. I am very good friends with the city editor of that newspaper. I think we should go down and surrender to him, tell him our side of the story. There is one thing about Bill Courtney you should know: He loves animals. He saw a man beating a pet bear at a livery stable over behind city hall and wrote an article about it. Next day, that big man came charging into the newspaper office and asked who had written that story about the bear. Bill Courtney took off his eyeshade, got up from behind his desk, and said he had done it, then promptly knocked the man down."

So that's what we did that late afternoon. We went down to the office of the Norfolk *Virginian-Pilot* and surrendered to Bill Courtney. It was a stroke of genius, because the story he wrote the next day made Calderham appear to be one of the most unfeeling officials around. Courtney was a fine writer, and even though I was involved, it almost brought tears to my eyes to read about the "outrageous" attempt to separate a "tragic orphan" from her dog, and the courageous actions by a boy and girl to prevent same. A picture of all three of us ran with the story, which ran for almost a full page, and no one could have read it dry-eyed.

Mrs. Crowe's phone rang most of the next day, and she seemed to be proud to be a part of it, as

did the railroaders. One phone call in the afternoon brought an offer from the Johnston Blue
Cross Lines to transport us to London, which
was immediately accepted. In no time at all, we
were in their commodious offices in the Century
Building on Granby Street to complete arrangements. Tee and Boo would go as passengers, as
usual, and I would join the crew as deck boy. Sailing in ten days, more or less. Mrs. Crowe gra-
ciously offered to *guest* us during that period.

Courtney's story had said that I felt duty-
bound to escort the British castaway girl to her
doorstep, and the Blue Cross line had noted that.
And, of course, I was now experienced from two
previous voyages.

24

I HAD SWORN I would never sail on a smoke-belching, steam-spouting coal burner, but there I was on the afterdeck of the SS *Plummer* as we singled up the lines on Monday, May 1, 1899, to commence the voyage to London, England. Tee was up on the boat deck with Boo, and down on the dock were about thirty people, well-wishers. Mrs. Crowe was down there with some of the railroaders and a few women from the railway auxiliary. Mr. Courtney was there, as was Mr. Jordan. Then, there were plain people who had heard about us or seen us on the streets. Notably missing was Consul Henry Calderham, who did not show his face around town very much these fine spring afternoons.

With a *Joseph Clark* tug lashed alongside to carry us out into the stream, we pulled the last lines aboard, and the *Plummer* retreated from the dock. Tee and I waved to all the helpful people who had come down to see us off. Then the ship began to quiver as the steam engine turned revolutions for the propeller. We let the tug go, and headed out to sea, passing several schooners and barks in Hampton Roads making sail for their voyages. I would not look at them, feeling somehow traitorous.

The *Plummer*, under command of Cap'n Stanislaus Johnson, whom I never formally met, was the largest ship I'd ever been on, at 412 feet; she carried a little over 5,000 tons of cargo. Down in her holds were 14,000 bushels of corn, 6,000-odd sacks of cottonseed meal, 4,000-odd sacks of oil cake, 140 cases of finished wagon spokes, several thousand loose oars, in addition to 16,000 sacks of flour and assorted carloads of hard- and softwoods.

Stem to stern, the *Plummer* had a stubby bow, then a well deck for No. 1 and No. 2 hatches, the bridge and officers' quarters (I never went inside them), smokestack next, under which were the boiler room and the engine room, then the crew's quarters, where I lived, and the galley. Two more cargo hatches were aft, then the stern works. Her engine was the up-and-down steam-cylinder type and pounded worse than the waves on Chicky beach.

In passing, I will say I met some new, modern types on the *Plummer*. They had "coal passers," who brought the coal to the front of the boiler fires for "stokers." These men filled their shovels from the coal passers' pile and threw the lumps evenly over the bed of fire, three fires in each boiler. It was hot and dirty down there, and, aside from looking once, I stayed away.

Having full intentions of returning to the joy of sail at the completion of this voyage back to America, I would not let myself be impressed with the *Plummer.* Yet I did enjoy the fact that she could make freshwater and we'd cross to London in nine or ten days.

Except for having to chip rust much of the time and paint the rest, my chores were not too different from those on the *Harriet B. Ritter.* They were anything the bosun made up his mind to do on any day: mop, scrub, holystone, etc.

There was one large difference in this vessel, and his name was James P. McGoffin, aged fifteen. He was another deck boy, out of Quincy, Massachusetts. Though he was not foreign, he certainly talked differently from anyone I'd ever heard. New England talk, I now know, and just as queer as the way some Bankers spoke, or more so. When Tee and I came aboard, he smiled with a row of Massachusetts teeth and said, "Howja do, call me Jimmy or Mac." To me, he was McGoffin, then and now. He had the midnight-to-four bridge-wing lookout watch, and I had the eight-to-twelve.

For some reason I've never been able to understand, Tee and the dog were true celebrities on that ship, while I was considered just another deck boy. Everyone had read the story in the *Pilot* and I was certainly well mentioned, but they seemed only to talk to Tee about it.

Throughout that first day, I saw the pretty blond up on the bridge talking to the captain, who otherwise seemed to spend all his time throwing a leather ball with the third mate over No. 2 Hatch. I saw the castaway on the boat deck talking to various officers. After we got squared away for sea and dropped the pilot, I chipped rust on the well-deck ladders aft but had a good view of the midships house. Several times, she also talked to McGoffin.

In late afternoon, she came back and we chattered for a little while, talking pleasantly about all the excitement in Norfolk. She asked me how I liked "Mac" and I said I could take him or leave him alone. She said she thought he was very nice and so good-looking. I didn't know him well enough to agree on the former and my eyes disagreed on the latter: He had a weak chin.

After supper on any ship is a time of relaxation to digest the meal and look at the sea and sunset, to think how nice it is to be out on the ocean rather than stuck on land, to thank the Lord for the fair weather. I had planned to spend some time with Tee that evening, but McGoffin got up from his plate first, scoured it off, and left the messroom. I had no idea what was on his mind.

By the time I got out to sit on the small hatch aft of the bridge, he had Tee by the rail, talking his head off, raking his fingers up and down Boo's back. Any dog will enjoy that. I walked on forward and sat down on the bitts at the bow, and watched the sun sink. It was a nice spring night. I stayed there until it was time for me to go up on the bridge wing and relieve the lookout. I paced the wing, thinking mostly about McGoffin, talking very little to the third mate, because he didn't have much to say to me.

Tee came up about nine-thirty (she seemed to have the run of the ship, including the officers' quarters), to say good night. Before saying that, she asked, "Ben, are you avoiding us?"

I said, "Nope, been busy today." Then I turned back to my job. I didn't want the *Plummer* running down some trawler.

Tee asked, "Are you angry because I've been talking to Mac?"

I laughed into the wind. "McGoffin? Why should I be?"

"He's been telling me so many things about Massachusetts."

"There's not much to tell about that state," I said.

Tee was silent a minute, then said, "I think you're jealous, Ben."

I laughed again. "How could I be jealous? There's nothing between you and me from all I could see and hear around this ship today. You talk to McGoffin as much as you want."

Tee answered, "All right, I will. He asked me if I'd be free when we got to London."

"You'll be all the way free," I said.

"Yes, and remember that," Tee answered, then trailed down the ladder with that dog, not even saying good night.

I yelled after her, "I'll make sure you're safe until midnight." A minute past then, there would be no guarantee: McGoffin had the lookout until 4 A.M.

She went on down to the main deck.

When McGoffin came up on the bridge, about ten to twelve, I noticed he was sleepy and blinking. It is usual practice for the twelve-to-four watch to catch a few hours' nap before coming up on the bridge. I said to him curtly, "A lot of traffic out here tonight," and went on to bed.

The second day was no better. I still had much rust to chip aft, and McGoffin had somehow got himself assigned to work midships. Almost every time I looked up, he was somewhere near her. Once, I saw him rubbing the back of her wrist. I had no idea what his intentions were but having brought her through storm and crisis for six months I was not about to let a fast talker from Quincy put her into jeopardy now.

Filene had once told me that you size any situation up but never let it go too long. You stay on top the wave and don't let it get on top you; you keep your bow into the waves and don't get sideways and broach. If you can't make up your mind and fiddle-faddle around, you sink.

That midnight, when McGoffin came up to relieve me, he was sleepy and blinking, having just come out of the lights in the crew's messroom. My eyes were lynx-sharp. I stayed away over near the outboard railing on the wing as he came that way. I waited until he was about two feet off, then kicked his feet out from under him and bent him over the rail so he was looking straight down to where boiling white sea was washing the *Plummer*'s iron plates.

I whispered into his ear, "I have nursed that girl along for six months from the brink of death, and you don't mess with her anymore. I aim to deliver her in London intact. Understand." That's all I said.

Just as I was letting him recover from his doubled-up position, weak chin pointed to at least eight hundred fathoms, the second mate walked out and asked, "What's going on here?"

Glancing at McGoffin, I could see his face was pale and drawn. I said, "Sir, Mac just lost his hat overboard and we were looking down for it."

The second shrugged. "I never saw Mac wear a hat." Then he walked on back into the bridge house.

I said, "Good night, McGoffin," and went below.

Next morning, I got to Tee as soon as I could and told her what I'd done and further told her to stop messing around with McGoffin.

Strange enough, she clapped her hands and said, "How lovely!"

Lovely was not involved.

Things got better after that, and aside from that deck boy from Quincy, it was a fine voyage.

So, in six more days, the *Plummer*, thudding steadily from her steam engine, belching steady smoke that spoiled the horizon astern for miles, pushing a white raft of water with her stubby bow, came abeam of the Scilly Islands and then Land's End, and proceeded on into the English

Channel. France lay ahead of us, but I wouldn't even think of that country. It wasn't visible, anyway, the weather being on the murky side.

We chugged on past such places as Portland Bill, St. Alban's Head, Brighton, and Folkestone, Tee calling them off though we could barely see the shore. I went about my work as she excitedly reported our progress. I had made progress myself and was now chipping rust on the forward well deck.

Finally, we rounded North Foreland and places called Ramsgate and Margate, picking up a sea pilot from a cutter, and then entered the mouth of the Thames River. That did give me a thrill. I had heard and read about that river for years, and now we were on it. There was as much traffic on that river, of a different kind, as there was on East Main Street in Norfolk. Ships and boats and barges of all types going in and out, both steam and sail.

I must confess, I wasn't doing much work. For every blow of that chipping hammer, I took five or ten looks. After we went through the waters of the Sea Reach, already beginning to approach the port of London on a flood tide, Tee said, "Over there are the low marshes of the Kentish coast, where Dickens's convict met Pip in *Great Expectations*." I had read that story. And there they were. Lordy.

Soon the banks of the Thames were filled with factories, and behind them I could see high church steeples. The size of this smoky city was beyond belief, because we hadn't even gotten close as yet.

A while later, the *Plummer* blew one long blast on her whistle and then four short ones. Tee said, "We're at Gravesend Reach, and we'll exchange the sea pilot for a river pilot." Sure enough, in a few minutes, a launch came alongside and the river pilot boarded. He was an old man but made the ladder ably.

"He's from the Trinity House Ruler of Pilots, oldest in the world. Founded by Henry VII in 1514," Tee said. That girl had a warehouse of information, and called it off as we churned steadily up the Thames, bending around at Northfleet

Reach and Gallions Reach. "We're eleven miles below London Bridge," she said. For a boy from the Outer Banks, it was almost too much.

I can't remember everything she said, but over there was Royal Albert Dock and King George V Dock and more railroad tracks than Mr. Riddleberger could have dreamt of. Threading through traffic of ships from every port in the world, we twisted and turned up the Thames, looping around at Bugsbys Reach into Blackwall and then into Greenwich Reach and Limehouse, all stretches of the great river.

Tee kept up her chatter, and it was of intense interest to learn that London had had many problems with thieves at one time. Organized river pirates that cut vessels loose from their moorings and ran them aground; night plunderers who went aboard ships during darkness with special overalls to fill their pockets; mud larks who stood in the mud at low tide while henchmen aboard threw goods over the side.

After the Limehouse stretch, we picked up a tug, and soon the *Plummer* was tied up at the

London docks, which Tee said were the harbor side of the Bank of England and Leadenhall Street. On up the river was London Bridge; then, bending on around, was Westminster Abbey and the Houses of Parliament. That May 10 was a memorable day in my life.

Some three hours later, after we had been cleared by customs and immigration, it was time for Tee and the dog to depart. Though it was busy aboard ship, the bosun allowed me thirty minutes off to say my farewells. In all the excitement of arrival, there had been little time to think that I had indeed safely delivered W. L. Appleton. Intact. I was proud of that.

Soon we stood on the dock, just talking a minute prior to her getting carriage transportation on to Belgravia and that four-story house filled with servants. She said she could get home very easily, and not to worry further. I said goodbye to her, and to Boo, having fulfilled everything.

But she lingered on to say, "Wouldn't you like to see where I live?" There was a certain glint in her blue eyes. Purpose in the way she stood. Boo sat beside her feet, peering around at merrie old England.

Fearing further involvement that might lead almost anywhere, I said, "Tee, you've told me all about that house, and I'm going to be very busy in this port. The bosun said that the only time I'll have free will be Saturday afternoon and Sunday. And I haven't made my plans for those days."

The glint seemed to grow. She said slowly, "Ben, would you not like to see the Tower of London, the changing of the guard at Buckingham Palace, the fish market at Billingsgate? Covent Garden? Ride on an omnibus and take a tunnel under the Thames? Go to a music hall . . ."

I gazed at her for a long time. Would it never end?

25

As I COMPLETE this account of a hectic period in my boyhood, when the Mother Sea was laughing at me dawn to dark, the year is 1914, and I'm in the weathered shingle-roof house that John O'Neal built at Heron Head, North Carolina.

I'm sitting at the oak table, off the wreck of the *Hermes,* in the same chair I occupied when Mama and I occasionally had a festive supper with Teetoncey back in the winter of '98 and '99. The chest off the *Minna Goodwin* is within eyesight, and Reuben's Mattamuskeet buck head is still on the north wall here in the front room. Not much has changed in this old house, and that has been on purpose. Our plot of hammock land also looks about the same, and that bent oak, on which a hooty owl perched the night I was born, still clings to its roots at the head of our pathway.

Despite everything that's happened in the outside world, and I've seen a lot of it now, not much has changed on our Outer Banks. Everyone goes about his or her way in a caring fashion. Of course, ships still crash on our shores in gales of wind, but more are steamers than sailing vessels. That, we can't control.

There have been changes of a human type, though. Reuben came home from the seas three years ago and is now a dirt farmer in Beaufort County, over near Mineola. Happily married, at last, he has a fine country-girl wife and baby daughter. He's quite content to grow crops and raise chickens and milk a Guernsey cow, staying out of earshot of the surf. I see him now and then.

Keeper Filene Midgett died a few years back on an ebb tide and is now peacefully buried in Chicky ground, not too far from Mama and the two crosses of Tee's parents, with *A* for Appleton on them. Filene can watch his beloved and equally feared Atlantic Ocean from his site, and surely does. Jabez Tillett now commands Heron Head Lifesaving Station, and in his own quiet way, between eight-foot spits of chewing plug, runs it well. Mark Jennette is the keeper down at Chicky station, though he swears he's going back to sea on a turbine ship.

Of no surprise, Kilbie Oden went to the university at Chapel Hill and is now in finance, threatening to copy old man Vanderbilt up North. Frank Scarborough is teaching school down in Hatteras village.

My life has changed some, too, naturally. After thirteen years of voyaging, and having reached second mate's papers, I came home, at least temporarily, ten months ago to assume second-in-command of Heron Head station. Jabez will be retiring from the Lifesaving Service in three years, and I suppose I'll follow along behind Filene and Jabez, and so many others before them.

The reason I came home is the old reason. I swore I wouldn't get married until forty or so, but found myself taking the vows in 1910. It was a wearing-down process by a very skillful girl. But I don't really regret being worn down into matrimony. She gave up some things, too.

She's out in the kitchen now, big as a small barrel with our second child. Our first was born two years ago, a boy. I'm not sure he looks like me, but we called him Ben, anyway. He gets around pretty well on short, strong legs; even down toward the muddy Pamlico and that old dock, which I'm now repairing in spare time.

Lucky that we've got a big yellow hound to keep watch on that two-year-old. That hound I "shared" with Tee passed on to canine heaven in 1908 and is buried in Belgravia. Probably the first Banks hound that ever had the distinction of going to his rest in such a fancy place. This Lab we've got now is called Hans, brought over from England. Old Boo contaminated the breed despite all. Hans will never be a duck dog like his papa was at one point, but he has other talents. His mistress tells everyone he's an "extra-aaaordinary guardian." So British.

I have to laugh about something else. Just a few minutes ago, Tee bundled the boy up, and he and Hans went off the steps and out into the yard. Tee called after them to say, "Now, don't go near the water, Benjamin," sounding just a little bit like the Widow O'Neal; such an echo from the past.

About the Author

Theodore Taylor

Acclaimed author Theodore Taylor was born in North Carolina and began writing at the age of thirteen, covering high school sports for a local newspaper. Before turning to writing full time, he was, among other things, a prizefighter's manager, a merchant seaman, a movie publicist, and a documentary filmmaker. The author of many books for young people, he is known for fast-paced, exciting adventure novels, including the Edgar Allan Poe award winner *The Weirdo; Air Raid—Pearl Harbor!;* and the bestseller *The Cay,* which won eight major literary awards, among them the Lewis Carroll Shelf Award. Mr. Taylor lives near the ocean in Laguna Beach, California.